AND

"What James Lee Burl[...] Hillerman for the Southwest, John Sandford for Minnesota, and Joe R. Lansdale for east Texas, Randy Wayne White does for his own little acre."

—*Chicago Tribune*

"White takes us places that no other Florida mystery writer can hope to find." —*Carl Hiaasen*

"White brings vivid imagination to his fight scenes. Think Mickey Spillane meets *The Matrix*." —*People*

"A major new talent . . . hits the ground running . . . a virtually perfect piece of work. He's the best new writer we've encountered since Carl Hiaasen."

—*The Denver Post*

"White is the rightful heir to joining John D. Mac-Donald, Carl Hiaasen, James Hall, Geoffrey Norman. . . . His precise prose is as fresh and pungent as a salty breeze." —*The Tampa Tribune*

"White doesn't just use Florida as a backdrop, but he also makes the smell, sound, and physicality of the state leap off the page." —*South Florida Sun-Sentinel*

"This satisfying madcap fare could go seismic on the regional bestseller lists." —*Publishers Weekly*

"He describes [...] so well it's easy to smell the salt [...] and feel the cool Gulf breeze." —*Mansfield News Journal*

CUBAN
DEATH-LIFT

Randy Wayne White

writing as Randy Striker

A SIGNET BOOK

SIGNET
Published by New American Library, a division of
Penguin Group (USA) Inc., 375 Hudson Street,
New York, New York 10014, USA
Penguin Group (Canada), 90 Eglinton Avenue East, Suite 700, Toronto,
Ontario M4P 2Y3, Canada (a division of Pearson Penguin Canada Inc.)
Penguin Books Ltd., 80 Strand, London WC2R 0RL, England
Penguin Ireland, 25 St. Stephen's Green, Dublin 2,
Ireland (a division of Penguin Books Ltd.)
Penguin Group (Australia), 250 Camberwell Road, Camberwell, Victoria 3124,
Australia (a division of Pearson Australia Group Pty. Ltd.)
Penguin Books India Pvt. Ltd., 11 Community Centre, Panchsheel Park,
New Delhi - 110 017, India
Penguin Group (NZ), 67 Apollo Drive, Mairangi Bay,
Auckland 1311, New Zealand (a division of Pearson New Zealand Ltd.)
Penguin Books (South Africa) (Pty.) Ltd., 24 Sturdee Avenue,
Rosebank, Johannesburg 2196, South Africa

Penguin Books Ltd., Registered Offices:
80 Strand, London WC2R 0RL, England

Published by Signet, an imprint of New American Library,
a division of Penguin Group (USA) Inc.

First Printing, February 1981
First Printing (Author Introduction), April 2007
10 9 8 7 6 5 4 3 2 1

Copyright © New American Library, a division of Penguin Group (USA) Inc.,
1981
Introduction copyright © Randy Wayne White, 2006
All rights reserved

 REGISTERED TRADEMARK—MARCA REGISTRADA

Printed in the United States of America

For those of us who made it out of Mariel

Introduction

In the winter of 1980, I received a surprising phone call from an editor at Signet Books—surprising because, as a Florida fishing guide, the only time New Yorkers called me was to charter my boat. And if any of my clients were editors, they were savvy enough not to admit it.

The editor said she'd read a story by me in *Outside Magazine* and was impressed. Did I have time to talk?

As a mediocre high school jock, my idols were writers, not ball players. I had a dream job as a light-tackle guide, yet I was still obsessed with my own dream of writing for a living. For years, before and after charters, I'd worked hard at the craft. Selling a story to *Outside*, one of the country's finest publications, was a huge break. I was about to finish a novel, but this was the first time New York had called.

Yes, I had time to talk.

The editor, whose name was Joanie, told me Signet

wanted to launch a paperback thriller series that featured a recurring he-man hero. "We want at least four writers on the project because we want to keep the books coming, publishing one right after the other, to create momentum."

Four writers producing books with the same character?

"Characters," Joanie corrected. "Once we get going, the cast will become standard."

Signet already had a template for the hero. He was a Vietnam vet turned Key West fishing guide, she said, talking as if the man existed. He was surfer-boy blond, and he'd been friends with Hemingway.

I am not a literary historian, but all my instincts told me the timetable seemed problematic. I said nothing.

"He has a shark scar," Joanie added, "and he's freakishly strong. Like a man who lifts weights all the time."

The guys I knew who lifted weights were also freakishly clumsy, so . . . maybe the hero, while visiting a local aquarium, tripped during feeding time?

My brain was already problem-solving.

"He lives in Key West," she said, "so, of course, he has to be an expert on the area. That's why I'm calling. You live in Key West, and I liked your magazine story a lot. It seems like a natural fit."

Actually, I fished out of Sanibel Island, on Florida's Gulf Coast, a six hour drive from Sloppy Joe's, but this was no time for petty details.

"Have you ever been to Key West?" I asked the editor. "Great sunsets."

Editors, I have since learned, can also be cagey. Joanie didn't offer me the job. She had already settled on three of the four writers, she said, but if I was willing to submit a few sample chapters on speculation, she'd give me serious consideration.

Money? A contract? That stuff was "all standard," she told me, and could be discussed later.

"I'll warn you right now," she said, "there are a couple of other writers we're considering, so you need to get at least three chapters to me within a month. Then I'll let you know."

I hung up the phone, stunned by my good fortune. My first son, Lee, had been born only a few months earlier. My much adored wife, Debra, and I were desperate for money because the weather that winter had been miserable for fishing. But it was *perfect* for writing.

I went to my desk, determined not to let my young family down.

At Tarpon Bay Marina, where I was a guide, my friend Ralph Woodring owned a boat with *Dusky* painted in big blue letters on the side. My friend, Graeme Mellor, lived on a Morgan sailboat named *No Mas*.

Dusky MacMorgan was born.

Every winter, Clyde Beatty-Cole Bros. Circus came to town. Their trapeze artists, I realized, were not only freakishly strong, but they were also freakishly nimble.

Dusky gathered depth.

One of my best friends was the late Dr. Harold Westervelt, a gifted orthopedic surgeon. Dr. Westervelt became the Edison of Death, and he loved introducing himself that way to new patients. His son, David, became Westy O'Davis, and our spearfishing pal, Billy, became Billy Mack.

Problems with my hero's shark scar and his devoted friendship with Hemingway were also solved.

Working around the clock, pounding away at my old black manual typewriter, I wrote *Key West Connection* in nine days. On a Monday morning, I waited for the post office to open to send it to New York.

Joanie sounded a little dazed when she telephoned on Friday. Was I willing to try a second book on spec?

Hell, yes.

God, I was beginning to *love* New York's can-do attitude.

The other three writers (if they ever existed) were fired, and I became the sole proprietor of Capt. Dusky MacMorgan—although Signet owned the copyright and all other rights after I signed Joanie's "standard" contract. (This injustice was later made right by a willing and steadfast publisher and my brilliant agent.)

If Joanie (a fine editor) feels badly about that today, she shouldn't. I would've signed for less.

I wrote seven of what I would come to refer to as "duck and fuck" books because in alternating chapters Dusky would duck a few bullets, then spend much-deserved time alone with a heroine.

Seldom did a piece of paper go into my old typewriter that was ripped out and thrown away, and I suspect that's the way the books read. I don't know. I've never reread them. I do remember using obvious clichés, a form of self-loathing, as if to remind myself that I should be doing my *own* writing, not this job-of-work.

The book you are now holding, and the other six, constituted a training arena for a young writer who took seriously the discipline demanded by his craft and also the financial imperatives of being a young father.

For years, I apologized for these books. I no longer do.

—Randy Wayne White
Cartagena, Colombia

1

In a foreign land, a land of aliens and alien politics, the killing becomes easier. The screams still haunt you, but the faces lose shape; dissipate like a sea fog at first light, and you become more and more a stranger—and the shadows become confidants. Separated from the reality of your country, your friends, your home, the newly dead become nothing more than obstacles on a path already followed, like beads on an abacus, or fears that have been conquered, and you know—with a pain like a white cold light—that you must keep killing, you must stay on the path, because it is forever and always the only way back. . . .

The day before my federal connection, Norm Fizer, told me about the disappearance of the three CIA agents in Mariel Harbor, Cuba, the squall hit.

The word "squall" doesn't seem strong enough to describe the storm that came roaring down unannounced from the open ocean of the west-northwest.

Winds gusting to ninety knots, seas walling ten to fifteen feet, death written all over the face of it. And the weather boys in southern Florida did a bad job of picking it up. A damn bad job. For them it meant just one more mistake to log with the others and forget. But for the thousands of Cuban-Americans in small boats bound for Mariel Harbor to pick up relatives in the largest Cuban sealift in history, it meant disaster.

It was a Sunday in late April. Normally, April is a time for recovery in Key West. The barrage of tourism is over by Easter, and the citizens of the little island city that has become America's chic dead end usually spend April walking the spent streets, blinking their eyes at the new quiet, at the return of the old slowness, like bears just out of hibernation.

But not this April.

You must have heard all about it, headline after headline, with film at eleven. The international newsmongers have turned us all into victims. We've become headline addicts, and they've increased our supply so gradually and steadily that we don't even realize the seriousness of our addiction. Most of us forget the dreams we've just had in the white glare of the morning edition, and at six we're too busy with Cronkite's understated lamentations to hear the words of our own children. The little man from Walden Pond saw the folly of that, but he was no anchorman, so who listens?

So you know about the Cubans who crashed the gate at the Peruvian embassy outside of Havana and demanded political asylum in early April. It was nothing new, really. Cubans tired of Castro's pipe dream had long ago figured out that breaking into the embassies of Peru and Costa Rica was the most reliable way out. But this time the unexpected happened. When the Peruvians, as always, refused to return the would-be refugees, Castro sent bulldozers to crash down the gates, removed his military force, and announced that anyone who wanted to abandon "the dream of socialism" was welcome to take refuge at the little embassy. Within two days, more than ten thousand Cubans had collected on the grounds. There was no food, so they ate the mangoes off the embassy tree, and then the leaves, and then the bark. The embassy's cat and guard dog were killed and roasted over an open fire. By the time the Peruvians—with the help of Costa Rica—had started to airlift refugees (fifty at a time) to South America, the world press got hold of the story, and Castro was made to look like the maniac he is. He might not care a hoot about the needs of his people, but he sure is sensitive to world opinion. He saw the refugees getting off the planes in Costa Rica as the source of his disgrace, so he found a way to halt the airlift— one of his goons pushed a Costa Rican diplomat through a plate-glass window. It wasn't an admirable method of diplomacy, but it was effective. The airlift was halted immediately. Then Castro did something which at the time seemed even stranger. He let it be known that if Americans wanted to come to Cuba by boat, they were welcome to pick up relatives—

whether they were among the thousands at the Peruvian embassy or not. At first it didn't make any sense. I followed the news reports, like everyone else in Key West, and couldn't figure it out. Why would Castro suddenly give his people the freedom of choice? And then I remembered something my little friend Carlos de Marti had told me. Carlos is in love with a Cuban woman—whom he had grown up with before his parents shipped him off to America in 1960. Once a month—if he can manage it—Carlos makes the dangerous ninety-mile crossing alone to visit his girl on a secluded beach, and then sneaks back, bringing with him two cases of Hatuey beer for me. After his last trip, he had told me the way things were in Cuba.

"Very bad, *amigo*," he had said. As always, he had brought the beer down to the docks at Garrison Bight in Key West where I moor my charter boat, *Sniper*. "My little love asked me if, on my next trip, I would consider bringing her and her family back. That is the only thing that keeps us apart—her family. But things are very bad there now and getting worse. Little bugs ruined the national sugarcane crop, and there is some blue fungus that has killed all the tobacco. At first it was a joke, see? No tobacco, so Fidel could no longer smoke his big Cohiva cigars. But then it was not so funny. There was no money, so there was no food. When starving people are caught stealing oranges from the national groves, they were imprisoned. My little love has gotten so thin, *amigo*, that I am worried. The next trip, she will come back with me—family or no family."

When I remembered that, it started to make more sense. American boats in Cuba would bring American dollars. And unloading poor Cubans would take some pressure off Castro's economy. When the first two boatloads of refugees came into Key West on April 21, I understood even further. I was out off Mule Key at the time, trying to chum up some bonefish for two doctors from Moline. The first boats back were two Miami lobster fishermen—the *Dos Hermanos* and the *Blanchie III.* I watched the Coast Guard escort them back to the submarine base beside the low, dun-colored geometrics of old Fort Taylor. The boats were pathetically overloaded. One of Castro's little jokes. Overload the American boats just to see how many would be lost on the dangerous crossing of the Florida Strait. And for all the people on those two boats, there weren't that many relatives of Cuban-Americans. For every three relatives Castro allowed to leave, he sent about twenty of his castoffs— the elderly, political prisoners, habitual criminals. Another of his little jokes. But the Cuban-Americans didn't care—and I couldn't blame them. Most of them still had mothers, fathers, sisters, and brothers back in Cuba, and it was their only chance to get them out. So they filed into Key West, thousands upon thousands, trailing their small fishing boats behind their cars, gas in plastic cans, food in coolers, ready to risk their lives to make the crossing and get their loved ones back. There wasn't enough hotel space on the island, so they slept in their cars and drank their morning coffee sitting on the curbs of sidewalks.

Yes, it was a strange April in Key West.

There were so many Cuban-Americans unloading their boats at Garrison Bight that the Sheriff's Department had to send deputies to direct traffic day and night. And the little harbor was packed. For those of us who had boats on charterboat row, it was a real pain in the butt. Most of them had little knowledge of seamanship, so they were constantly running over anchor lines and ramming into wharves and other boats, occasionally catching fire. It was a deadly serious kind of Keystone Kops. It got so that the other guides and I were afraid to leave our boats unguarded. When you came in from a charter, there were normally two or three Cuban-American boats in your slip, and it wasn't easy getting them to move. There were people and noise and traffic everywhere, so finally I just said to hell with it.

And that's how I happened to be out in my stilthouse off Calda Bank when the squall hit.

It's some kind of place to watch a squall come in. It's an old fisherman's shack, built in open water eight feet deep, and the nearest land is Fleming Key—about a mile or so away. The old pine clapboard is a weathered gray, and the roof is tin. The sixteen pilings it's built on are stout and smell of creosote, and they angle down into the clear water where barracuda hang in the shadows and big gray snapper swim their nervous figure eights. I had bought the stilthouse only a few months before. I wanted solitude, and I had the money—more money than I could use in a lifetime, after that deadly last mission off the Marquesas. I had plenty to forget, and I was tired of the strange April madness that had overtaken Key West.

I wanted to be alone, to rest, to forget. And there is no place on earth better for being alone than a stilthouse.

On the Friday before the squall, I ambled up to the marina at Garrison Bight and told Stevie Wise to cancel all my charters until the craziness was over. Stevie looked harried and weary, which isn't hard to understand, really. He lives on an old lunker of a houseboat named *Fred Astaire*, which is as famous around Key West for its parties as Stevie is well known for his enthusiastic bachelorhood. But it was neither women nor parties which had exhausted him. It was the madness of what the newspapers were calling the Freedom Flotilla.

We stood in the little marina office staring out at the wild activity in the harbor. Cars with boats on trailers sat in a long line down Roosevelt Boulevard, waiting in the April heat to unload at the cement ramp. Fifty or sixty other boats were rafted in the harbor, while others tried to anchor with knotted lines, old engines smoking, their skippers screaming Spanish insults at each other.

"I can't believe they're letting this crap go on," Stevie said. He had taken the phone off the hook to stop the endless barrage of calls he had been getting from the country's news media, and he sat behind the counter on a wooden stool.

"Come on, Steve—you'd be going too if you had relatives trapped in Cuba."

"No, it's not that." He brushed at his thick black hair with a free hand. With the other, he toyed with a pencil. "What I can't believe is that they're letting those poor people head across the Strait in those damn little boats. Look out there! What are they, mostly eighteen-to-twenty-three-footers? Shit, that's suicide."

"You've got to admire their bravery. They're a determined people."

"Yeah, determined to get themselves killed. I don't see why they all just don't hire shrimp boats—or licensed captains like you—to take them across. Makes a helluva lot more sense."

"Stevie, you know what those shrimp-boat people are charging—and if you don't, you ought to walk on down and have a beer at the Kangaroo's Pouch. That's where all the dealing's going on. The shrimp boats are getting between fifty and a hundred thou in cash for a trip. And that's in advance—with no guarantees. And the reason I'm not going is that no one I know has asked. The Cuban-Americans I do know are close friends, and I suppose they just don't want to put me on the spot."

"And what if they did ask?"

I thought for a moment. Would I go? Castro was making a fool of everyone who went to Mariel Harbor, no doubt about that. He was making a fool of Americans, his own people—everyone but himself. But the bottom line was that there were good people who looked upon this sealift as their only chance to rescue their relatives from Castro's little commie paradise. Some paradise.

Stevie stared at me with his mocking brown eyes and began to grin. "If one of your friends asked, you'd be gone in a minute, MacMorgan. You know it's true."

I snorted. Maybe it was. And maybe that's why I had decided to isolate myself on my stilthouse—to escape being asked. I didn't want to haul Castro's castoffs, so I was taking the coward's way out. You don't have to make any decisions when the world can't find you. And I was tired of decisions. I wanted to sit in my little weather-scoured shack on the sea, drink cold beer, read good books, and catch fish— just to let them go and watch them swim free again. Key West could have its traffic and its Mariel Harbor madness. And it could have it without me.

I finished rescheduling my charters, shoved the long black calendar back under the counter, and turned to leave. As I did, Stevie stopped me.

"Hey, Dusky—I almost forgot." He began shuffling through a stack of papers on a metal spindle. "You got a message here someplace. . . ."

"It'll keep."

"Naw, the guy said it was very important. Had nothing to do with a charter—hey, here it is."

I took the narrow envelope he handed me and

opened it. It was from Norm Fizer. Stormin' Norman
we had called him on one very secret mission a long,
long time ago back in Cambodia. I had been a Navy
SEAL back then, more fish than man, more killer
than fish. It was a dirty, nasty, dangerous time, but
I had come to respect and admire Fizer during our
mission there. He's a fed—and one of the rare good
ones. I owed him a lot—and not just because of Cambodia. When the drug runners—the pirates who
roam the Florida Strait and call Key West home—
made the mistake of murdering my family and my
best friend, Norm had seen to it that I had the chance
to get even. He had hired me as a government free-
lance troubleshooter, working outside the law to ex-
pedite the work of the lawkeepers.

The note read:

Dusky,
Wanted to congratulate you again on the
Marquesas affair. Well done. May have something else for you. Since you moved off *Sniper*,
I don't know where you are staying so it is
important you call me at the Atlanta number as
soon as possible.

NF

It was typed in plain block pica, just typed initials
for a signature. So it was business. But I wasn't ready
for any more business. Not now, anyway. I had been
having a bad time of it since that brutal night off the
little chain of mangrove islands called the Marquesas.

At night I couldn't sleep, and during the day I couldn't seem to wake up. I was drinking too much beer, and my hands shook slightly when I tied new leaders. That's what killing does to you. It steals into the middle of your brain and begins to eat its way out again. I needed more time to shake it, to put it all behind me, to crush the nightmares in the peace of isolation.

I crumpled the note and jammed it into the pocket of my khaki fishing shorts.

"You never gave me this."

"What? Huh?" Stevie had a swatter in his hand, and he was swinging at a luminous deerfly that buzzed its complaints about the invention of glass windows.

"Do me a favor, Steve, and play along."

He gave me an unconcerned shrug. "Captain MacMorgan hasn't been in today, sir. Sorry, I don't know where he's living."

Outside, I nudged my thirty-four-foot sportfisherman out of her berth, feeling the sweet sync of her twin 453 GM diesels bubbling me over the clear green water of the harbor. I had an icy Hatuey beer in a Styrofoam hand-cooler, a pinch of Copenhagen snuff wry in my lower lip, and as I piloted from the flybridge, I tried to recapture the delight I usually felt in going out to sea alone.

But it didn't work. I couldn't get the muscles in my shoulders to relax, and it seemed as if I looked out onto the world, through glazed eyes. I dropped *Sniper* into dead idle as I came up behind four ratty fiberglass fishing boats loaded with gas cans, boxes of food, and determined Cuban-Americans, all heading out Garrison Bight Channel, bound for the wicked Florida Strait. The guy running the point boat couldn't have been more than eighteen. He had a tired outboard, belching smoke as it struggled to push the little skiff onward. The kid was shirtless, there was a smile on his face. But in the depths of my despair, it seemed as though a raven-shaped shadow haloed his head, diving and soaring, and the shadow was death. . . .

2

The storm came funneling out of the west-northwest across open sea. I watched it from the porch of the stilthouse, morning coffee in hand, noting the way the strange light which accompanied it changed from copper to bile green as it approached landfall.

And I knew that it was to be no ordinary squall.

I had spent the previous day, Saturday, trying to work some of the rough edges off the stilthouse—and myself. It's really a fairly large place for a house built on pilings out on the water. I went to work on the bedroom first. It only has one. I got rid of the old cot, and laboriously carried the wide double bed I had just bought and transported out on *Sniper*. The stilthouse faces south and north—with long porches on either side—and I set the bed up by the eastward window of my new quarters. The bedroom has a big brown oval of rag rug on the plank floor; it smelled musky and doggy, and I decided to keep it right where it was because I like dogs. I swept and cleaned and tacked black shades up so I could dark-out the bedroom if need be, and I built rough bookcases and transferred my small—but good—ship's library to the stilthouse. It felt good to be doing mindless work; work that required just enough thought to match the light sweat that the labor required. There wasn't much I could—or wanted to—do with the little galley and living area. There is an ancient stove and a small refrigerator, both of which run on bottled gas, and there is a sink with a faucet hooked up to the big five-hundred-gallon rooftop rain cistern that serves the little shower on the narrow dock built under the stilthouse. The man I had bought the place from—he had helped his father build it back in the 1930s as a place to store ice and supplies for the fishing boats—had left the giant shell of a loggerhead turtle on the wall, two sets of big mako jaws, a gas-station calendar from 1956 showing a blonde with improbable breasts, and four kerosene lamps hung in strategic spots. I filled them, changed wicks, then set about stringing fifty feet of copper wire outside the stilthouse to serve as an antenna for my portable Transoceanic shortwave receiver.

By dusk I had worked enough and sweated enough and relaxed enough to be pleased with my new home. After the death of my wife and sons I had taken up residence aboard *Sniper*. But *Sniper* was built and outfitted to stalk the Gulf Stream for the big ones, not to serve as an apartment for a guy who is six-two and a shade and weighs 220 pounds.

So this new place would be just fine. With its high

ceiling and location on the water it would be cool in the summer, and with the little oil stove, it would be fairly warm in winter.

As a final touch, I hung a Wellington Ward print of a wood ibis in flight, and one of Gustav Ameier's fine horizonless seascapes on the wall at a level where I could look at them when I wanted, then went out and swam the half mile to Calda Channel's marker 22. On the way back I took it slow, so Saturn had thrown its narrow white starpath across the open sea above the furtive blinking of channel markers to the west by the time I had my fish supper cooking and sat back in the overstuffed chair by kerosene lamp to read and listen to the radio.

The world news was filled with talk of the Mariel Harbor exodus.

I opened my sixth beer of the day, took up A. J. McClane's excellent *New Standard Fishing Encyclopedia* for the thousandth time, sat back and listened.

The BBC focused on the inexperience of most of the Cuban-Americans making the trip, and on the dangerous condition of the boats they were taking.

Radio Germany detailed the ambiguity of Jimmy Carter's pretending to welcome the refugees with "open heart, open arms" while his administration threatened the people making the trip with heavy fines and confiscation of their boats.

Radio Moscow, the announcer's voice bland and without any trace of accent, claimed that the refugees were being mistreated, starved, and even tortured upon their arrival in the United States.

Feeling the relentless political maneuvering of international affairs restoke the grayness within me, I spun the dial and came up with the marine weather report. The reporter always sounds as if he is speaking from the depths of some cave, walls covered with charts and figures and military weather graphs. It sounds like a voice in which to have confidence—and usually it is. But people who don't really know the sea can forget how lethal it can be to have complete faith:

Weather for Key West and vicinity through noon tomorrow: mostly clear with a sixty percent chance of precipitation, seas two to four feet inside the reef, four to six outside the reef. Line of heavy thunder showers moving east-southeast approximately one hundred miles off Cape Romano, but expected to weaken by morning. . . .

I flipped off the Transoceanic feeling the old grayness move upon me in a wave. Sooner or later, a storm would hit. And most of the poor bastards out there bound for Cuba didn't know the difference between a cement block and a Danforth—let alone how to ride out a bad squall in a small boat.

Sooner or later, some of them would go down.

And on whose hands would their blood be?

Castro's? Carter's? Their own?

Or those of us who took the coward's way out and watched with the same aloof interest we give the six-o'clock news, safe and secure in our isolation?

The squall came pounding across open sea, headed for Key West, dragging its tentacles of veiled rain and waterspouts like some kind of giant man-o'-war.

It was about nine a.m.; the day was overcast, just waiting for something to happen.

When I saw it coming, I dumped my morning coffee with a throwing motion, ran barefooted back into the stilthouse to see if anyone knew just how bad this one was going to be.

They did.

But too late.

The weather people were giving frantic updates, telling all boaters to head immediately for port.

Severe squall lines now approaching Key West and vicinity, winds expected at eighty knots or more, seas outside the reef twelve to fifteen feet . . .

It was going to be one roaring bastard, all right. I pulled some shorts on, ran back outside, and ripped off the clove hitches holding *Sniper* to the lee side of the dock. I shoved her off, hustled forward, and fired up both engines. I wanted her well away from the stilthouse when that brute hit. About four hundred yards away, I found about twelve feet of water on the flats. I broke out the extra anchor from the stern locker, nosed *Sniper* toward the storm and dropped the first, then drifted downwind at about thirty degrees and dropped the second, popping her astern as I did. I played out two hundred feet of line, still backing, then switched her off when I felt them bite. It was more than twice as much scope as she probably needed—but this was no ordinary squall.

Hand over hand, I pulled in the little Whaler skiff I had tethered astern, then pounded my way back to the stilthouse. It was already starting to sprinkle.

Only once in my life have I ever seen a squall like that, and that was in the South China Sea. But then I was on one of the big Triton boats and it was a simple matter of submerging to 120 feet and riding it out. Like that one, this squall came pounding down out of nowhere, hurricane-force winds kicking the crap out of everything in its way.

I battened down all the windows in the stilthouse, tied the door closed, got a beer, and then sat down in my reading chair to wait it out, smelling the rainy coolness and lightning in the wind.

There was nothing else I could do.

The surly old guy who had sold me the place had told me the way it would be in a bad storm. And he was right. The old stilthouse weaved and rocked in the wind, but she was solid as a ship, even when the waves began to break over the dock, slashing at the pilings.

There was no gentle pitter-patter of rain upon tin roof. The water roared down, thousands and thousands of gallons of it in a silver sky falls: the wind screamed and ripped, and lightning cracking at open sea actually sounded meek and hollow in comparison.

Just before the peak of it, I ran out to bail out the Whaler, and almost got carried away by the wind in the process. I came back in, soaking, pulled off my shorts, grabbed a towel, then sat back down and, almost reluctantly, switched on the Transoceanic.

I knew what I was going to hear.

And no one could look forward to that.

On VHF, the Coast Guard was being besieged by distress calls. The poor bastard at the mike couldn't log them fast enough—and almost all of them were in frantic Spanish or broken English.

Mayday, mayday, we're sinking, Mother of God . . .

If you have ever heard the voice of someone truly terrified, you never forget it. The voice seems to be laced with some potent edge which hits you like a drug and goes right to your spine. And the people on the radio begging for help were terrified. Hundreds of them. There was nothing orderly about their pleas for help. There was a chaos of voices, one distress call overlapping another, all broken by the static of lightning and the roar of the wind. It was all too easy to picture the way it would be out there in the bottomless sea of the Florida Strait. There would be that strange green squall light, and waves cresting eighteen feet high. Rain would be flooding down, slashing their desperate faces with the velocity of arrows, and they would be out there in their damn small boats—overloaded with food or fuel or refugees—as powerless as leaves in the centrifuge of storm and bleak sea.

Those that didn't broach would probably go awash or pitchpole. Engines would flood, electrical systems would short, and the wicked wave surge would snap arms and legs like dry twigs.

I listened to the stuttered, desperate cries for help on the VHF and knew there wasn't a damn thing I could do.

These were the victims. Innocent people who just

wanted to go to Cuba and rescue their relatives. They hadn't planned on getting caught in a death squall.

But the squall wasn't the culprit.

The politicians were.

I reached over and flipped off the Transoceanic, almost knocking it off the little stand beside my chair. I stood up, paced around the small area of the stilthouse. The tin roof was leaking in three or four places, and I stuck cooking pots beneath the leaks, then caulked window seals with towels.

One bastard of a storm.

With nothing else to do, I stooped and got another beer out of the little gas refrigerator, noticing, as I lifted it to my lips, that my hands were shaking.

Norm Fizer, my federal connection, arrived the next morning, by helicopter of all things. He stood on a pontoon after he landed and waved for me to come and get him.

The turquoise flats off the stilthouse were roiled and murky after the storm, but the day was clear, April warm. Nature has a way of showing its prettiest face after a tantrum. I loosed the little Boston Whaler, buzzed out, and picked him up.

Norm looks like a pro quarterback who was smart enough to slip into the world of corporate business before some linebacker ruined his good looks. He's like a Rockwell hybrid: Clint Eastwood and Jack Armstrong blended into a three-piece suit.

Amazingly, he wore a suit now.

He climbed down into the Whaler carrying a brief-case, wide face crinkled into a grin.

"You're damn hard to get in touch with these days, MacMorgan."

"Phone company just won't run a line out here, Norm."

He eyed me as we headed back toward the stilt-house. *Sniper*, painted blue-black, stood out dark against the gray of tin roof, the gray of weather-bleached shack, the gray of the horizon after a storm. The sea was flat and calm, yellow and then cobalt with the morning sun.

"You wouldn't be trying to hide from an old friend like me, would you, Dusky?"

"Bingo."

"What makes you so sure this is a business visit?"

I snorted. "Well, if it wasn't that college-boy suit you're wearing, the briefcase would tell me, and if it wasn't the briefcase, the helicopter might give you away. Don't you think that's a tad gaudy, Stormin' Norman?"

"I wanted to tie balloons and streamers to it, but the guys at the Boca Chica airbase wouldn't let me." He grew serious then. "But you're right, Dusky. It is business. Damn important business."

I held my hand, stopping him. "Not interested, Norm. Not yet. But you can have some coffee and make your pitch before I turn you down."

Norm said he liked my new home. He roamed around looking at this, asking questions about that, then stopped by my portable shortwave receiver. He sipped at his mug of coffee. "You were never much for news, Dusky. What's the story—you keeping up with the Mariel Harbor thing?"

"It's become kind of a hobby. I want to see how many people Castro and our own dear President let drown before they work out a sensible way to sealift those refugees—or stop it all together."

Norm lowered his head as if in some way—because he worked for the federal government, maybe—he carried some share of the burden.

"It's a damn messy situation, no doubt about that." He looked up again. "Did you hear the latest?"

"What's that?"

"Yesterday the Cuban authorities forced an American shrimp boat to leave the port of Mariel just before the storm hit. The boat was loaded with refugees—probably close to two hundred. Our Coast Guard monitored a distress call from the shrimp boat. Cuban authorities refused to go to their rescue—didn't even acknowledge the call. By the time one of our Coast Guard cutters got on the scene there wasn't a trace of anybody or anything. We figure it went down, all hands and all refugees lost."

"Jesus Christ. And they still can't find half the other boats they got distress calls from."

"No way of knowing who made it, who didn't. No way of even knowing how many boats and people were out there—a lot of them didn't even have radios. And they don't exactly register before leaving Key West. Like I said, Dusky . . . damn messy."

"And it makes no sense. The whole goddam thing makes no sense."

"It makes more sense than you think, Dusky. To Castro and . . . and to us."

I stopped and gave him a hard look. "What's that supposed to mean?"

He swirled the coffee in his mug. "Tell you what. Why don't you and I get some more coffee, sit down, and I'll tell you the whole story from beginning to end. And then if you still want to refuse to help, you can. But we need you, you big scarred-up bastard. Doesn't it feel good to be needed?"

"Sure," I said. "Yeah. It makes my heart feel about as warm as the blade of this knife I got strapped to my belt. . . ."

3

"First of all," Norm Fizer said, "Castro has some obvious reasons for wanting this sealift."

He sat straddling a chair, his jacket off, a fresh mug of coffee in his hand. From beneath us, from the moving sea, came the sound of a running tide bubbling around the pilings, and the snap and muted crackle of pistol shrimp within their tunicate hideaways.

"Money's got to be a big part of it," I said.

Norm nodded. "Absolutely. When Castro took power, he screwed up the country's entire economic system by abandoning the big money standbys—sugarcane and tobacco—and trying to diversify. He tried different crops, and he tried to industrialize before his people were ready for it. It got the country in such big financial trouble that he was forced to go back to what Cuba had always relied on—cane and tobacco. And things didn't go too badly then. But that first mistake got him deep in debt to the Moscow boys. Remember, Castro wasn't any worse than Batista at first—which is bad enough. But it wasn't anything compared to the kind of dictator he became when Russia got its puppet strings on him."

"That much I already know. Why don't you get to why you're here?"

He smiled. "For a guy who's trying to become a hermit, you sure as hell don't have much patience."

"It's the low wages." Animated, I pretended to check my watch. "Besides, I got bird watching at ten, a communing with nature at eleven, and a conversation with God at—"

"Okay, okay. Jesus, MacMorgan, you've become a sarcastic bastard, you know that?" He grinned when he said it.

"It's been a big year for sarcasm."

I shouldn't have put it that way. It sounded thankless. But when I did I realized the source of the depression which had been trailing me lately. Self-pity. I had been carrying it around on my sleeve. Like a scar. Or a cause. Or maybe even a medal. Self-pity is the most disgusting—and costly—of all indulgences, and I was immediately pissed off at myself for having said it. But Norm just took it in stride the way any good officer would.

"So I'll hurry."

"Maybe you ought to kick me in the ass first. I just realized that that's probably what I need."

He rubbed his chin with a big hand. "I know that the last twelve months must seem like a nightmare. . . ."

"Hey, let's forget it. The last person I should try to take it out on is you. You've done a lot for me, Stormin' Norman, and I appreciate it. I really do."

That All-American boy face of his was sober for a moment, then was transformed by masculine good humor. "Hey, you saved my tail once yourself—remember?"

"I thought we'd been ordered never to discuss that."

He winked. "I won't tell if you don't. But let's get back to this Cuban thing before committing any more treason. Huh?"

So Castro wanted the American boats in Mariel Harbor to make money. According to Norm, that was one reason—but not the most important. Castro was charging American captains outlandish rates for anchorage, food, beer, water, fuel, and repair.

"We figure Cuba is clearing about a half million dollars in cash for every day this thing goes on," Norm said. "And that's not counting the value of the boats they've confiscated for one reason or another. Now, the next obvious reason Castro wants this sealift to continue is that it's a hell of a chance to get rid of some of Cuba's excess human baggage. They're short on food over there, damn short on money, so he's sending us the people he doesn't want to support anymore. It looks like we're getting a lot of his mentally ill. And he's cleaning out the prisons—

sending them all over here. Now, it's true that a lot of his 'criminals' have done nothing worse than steal a mango or two—or try to escape to America. And those people will probably do fine here in the States. But others are the habitual criminals—murderers, rapists, scum like that. Castro's a shrewd bastard, you have to give him that. Because the murderers and the rapists aren't the worst of what he's sending."

"I think I can see where you're going with this."

"You're right. It's pretty obvious. He's slipping a hell of a lot of agents in on us, along with his criminals. How many refugees have landed in Key West so far? Thirty thousand or so. And they say there are at least a hundred thousand more coming. Our major source of secret information in Cuba tells us that about one in every five hundred refugees will be an agent. A Cuban agent who has been educated and trained in the Soviet Union, sent here to spy, carry out subversive activities, and generally raise hell."

"If you know who they are, why don't you just stop them at the docks and send them packing?"

"Because we *don't* know who they are. Not yet. But we will."

Fizer started to open his briefcase, stopped, stood up, and pretended to study the drawings on the wall.

"Hey, Norm," I said. "Why don't you cut the lecture on Cuban political history and get down to it?"

He came back and took his seat. He looked worried. Damn worried. And Stormin' Norman Fizer isn't a man to show emotion.

"Okay, Dusky. Here it is, blow by blow. First of all, at this very moment we've got about eight to ten thousand American civilians sitting over there in Mariel Harbor. Private citizens on private boats like sitting ducks in Cuban waters—enemy waters. If, for some wild reason, the Cubans wanted hostages they could seal off that bottleneck harbor with one small gunboat." He snapped his fingers. "With that many hostages, they could bring this country to its knees like that."

"But why in hell would the Russians let Castro even think of something so crazy?"

"Never mind *why* it might happen," Fizer snapped. "Let's just say that it could." He stopped, opened his briefcase, took out an envelope marked "Top Secret" and handed me a sheet of paper. "Ten days ago, for reasons you are about to learn, the CIA sent three of its best agents to Mariel Harbor. They are all Cuban by birth, so it was easy enough for them to pose as American civilians interested in applying for the release of relatives. You'll find their names and biographies listed there.

"The most obvious reason for having CIA agents in Mariel is to keep an eye on how our people are being treated. But there's another reason, too. I mentioned that we have a source of secret information in Cuba. Well, it is a very, very valuable source. It's one of the only sources we have, frankly. Do you remember when Castro visited the United Nations a few years ago?"

"Sure. Tightest security precautions taken for one man in the history of the country, or something—

right? Made a lot of Americans mad to think we took better care of a dictator than we do of our own Presidents. What about it?"

"That's when we made our first contact with a General F.C. Halcón, one of the top men in Castro's army. Since then his code name has been Hawk. And Hawk has proved invaluable to us. He's fairly representative of a growing disenchantment with Castro in Cuba—even among the higher-ups. The last report we got from him informed us of the agents being planted among the refugees, but it also contained the words—in code, of course—'storm nest.' That was his predetermined way of telling us he wanted out; things were getting hot for him, and he wanted us to get his ass out of Cuba."

I said, "Not all that easy, I imagine."

Norm shrugged and toyed with his coffee cup. "Normally, no. But it so happened that Halcón was assigned to run security operations in Mariel Harbor. So, three days after receiving his message, the CIA sent its agents in a forty-foot trawler, renamed *Storm Nest*, with orders to evacuate the Hawk."

"And what happened?"

Fizer looked up at me, the concern in his face obvious. "The CIA's people just disappeared. Vanished. Through a pretty complex code system, they got word to the Key West marine operator that they had arrived, and they were awaiting contact from the Hawk. And then *poof*, nothing."

"Maybe Castro's people were on to the whole operation and rounded up all four of them."

"That's what we figured at first, but four nights ago we got another code transmission from Halcón. He's anxious as hell to get out and can't figure why we haven't sent anyone to get him. That's why I'm here, Dusky."

"Hold it," I said. "I want a beer in my hand before I listen to this."

Fizer gave me that college-boy grin. "Jesus, Mac-Morgan, you act like I'm some sort of flimflam man or something."

"Or something," I agreed. I put an unrequested bottle of Hatuey on the table in front of him, then sat back down with my own, feeling the malted carbonation of the beer sluice away the acid taste of coffee.

"Dusky, we want you to take another of the CIA's agents to Mariel Harbor. A fine officer, a Lieutenant Santarun—another Cuban by birth, and supposedly one of the CIA's best people."

"I only work alone, you know that, Norm—and that's not to say I'm even considering—"

"Just listen for a minute, dammit! We just want you to take Santarun over there. The lieutenant will do the rest. I just want you to watch and listen, and give me your impressions when you get back. For your own protection, we're not even telling Santarun that you're one of our people. And you are never to let on that you know who Santarun is. All you have to do is play the role of the slightly stupid charterboat captain—and then report back."

I watched him for a moment. He toyed with his

beer—hardly touched—nervously. "You're a bad liar, Fizer. Does Santarun know that you're using him for bait?"

Fizer's dark eyes caught mine. "It was the lieutenant's idea, Dusky. Something's going on down there in Mariel Harbor, and we have to know what it is. If Castro's people knew beforehand that we were sending agents, it means that the CIA has a serious security breach to deal with. And if there is a breach, they'll come after Santarun, too. You're our ace in the hole, Dusky. They'll rig some way to get the lieutenant—some way that will probably seem innocent enough—then send you packing. They're not going to waste their time with a civilian. And that's all you'll be in their eyes—and in the eyes of Santarun. It's risky, you're right. But not for you. Like I said, it was the lieutenant's idea. We have to know, once and for all, if Castro's goons snatched our agents—"

"Norm—"

"—because, if they did—"

"Norm—"

"—we'll have to pick up a couple of theirs and start—"

"Norm, you're still not telling me everything, dammit!"

He stared at me in mild surprise. Boyish. A "What, me?" kind of innocence.

I knew that look. I'd seen it before. Back in an attack assignment in the jungles of Southeast Asia where no American was ever supposed to be. I leaned forward, bracing my elbows on the table between us. "Norm, old buddy, I was raised in the circus, remember? I grew up with the ten-in-one-show gypsters, the fire eaters, the magicians, and the backlot crapshooters. Don't try to con a carnie, Norm. I learned to recognize a scam before I learned the Pledge of Allegiance. There's a big chunk of your story missing, old buddy. Why not just tell me straight?"

"Tell you what?" The mock innocence was gone, replaced by a somber, searching look.

"Tell me who else might have snatched those three CIA people. I mean, if they've turned up missing, why not just *assume* it was Castro's people? Our people sure as hell just didn't sink in Mariel Harbor with fifteen hundred other boats anchored around them, did they? You're not telling me something, Stormin' Norman. The CIA isn't going to take the chance of losing another good agent just to prove a point. So why not tell your old friend Dusky who else might have grabbed the agents?"

He stood up and walked across the room, draining his beer in long, thoughtful swallows. The planks of the stilthouse creaked beneath the solid weight of him.

"That's all I'm supposed to tell you, Dusky."

I shrugged. "So get yourself another boy. I'm not going into this thing with blinders on."

"It's for your own good—"

"Horsecrap!"

He studied me momentarily, and then the grin returned. "Sometimes, MacMorgan, you're a little too smart for your own good."

"We hermits do a lot of reading."

He sat back down, all business now. "Okay, you asked for it. But you have to promise that you'll play dumb with Santarun—it could get you both killed. Okay? When the CIA first realized its agents had vanished, it was pretty much—as you said—assumed that the Cuban authorities had gotten hold of them. And just when the CIA was about to raise holy hell about it, this Lieutenant Santarun came up with a very interesting alternative explanation for their disappearance."

"And that is?"

Norm leaned back in his chair, measuring his words. He said, "It's just possible that the three agents weren't snatched at all. It's just possible that they disappeared of their own free will."

"Double agents? All three of them?"

Fizer shook his head. "Worse than that, I'm afraid. It's just possible that they've turned renegade. And the more I think about it, the more plausible it seems. No one hates the Castro regime more than our own Cuban-Americans. CIA agents or not. They could have gone to Mariel Harbor, abandoned their orders to try to evacuate General Halcón, and disappeared into the backcountry to regroup and carry out some kind of private commando operations. I don't have to tell you the immediate effect that would have on the eight or ten thousand Americans waiting in Mariel. Any act of war by those agents would make the members of the Freedom Flotilla prisoners—and damned unpopular prisoners at that."

I said, "So in a way you're actually hoping this Lieutenant Santarun will be snatched?"

"I know it seems crazy to hope that the CIA does have some kind of security leak, but we are. That will be a hell of a lot easier to deal with. But either way, we have to find out. We have to know for sure."

There was still something else on Fizer's mind, but he didn't need any nudging now. I gave him time, and after a thoughtful moment he said:

"Do you know what we're scared of, Dusky? If those agents have turned renegade, we're afraid that they're going for the biggest game of all. And if they succeed, it'll mean there are going to be a hell of a lot of bodies floating around Mariel Harbor. American bodies. And maybe even a world war. Dusky, we're afraid those agents have plans to assassinate Fidel Castro. . . ."

4

I first got suspicious of the television film crew when they followed me from the fuel docks down to the old submarine base at Trumbo Annex.

Two Cuban-looking guys. The one shouldering the camera pack was the bigger of the two. Black hair combed back. Open shirt with gold chains and unicorn horns curving through the thatch of black chest hair. A snappy dresser who didn't spend enough time looking through his viewfinder. He spent too much time eyeing me as I topped off my tanks with diesel fuel and loaded on the big blocks of ice for the long trip to Mariel Harbor.

So Fizer had finally convinced me.

Three agents might have gone bad. They might have shelved their duties to get a chance at putting a bullet through Fidel's beard. Or maybe there was just a rotten egg in the hallowed halls of the CIA.

Either way, I had spent the afternoon after Norm

buzzed off in his whirlybird battering myself with recriminations. Why in the hell had I given in so easily? I played with the idea of trying to back out; supported the idea with the rationale that I was letting Fizer's little super-secret organization of trouble-shooters run my life.

After all, when had he called that I hadn't jumped to answer?

Not since the nasty job on Cuda Key—and that is never.

So I had spent a tawny, late day in April getting the stilthouse squared away, storing this, locking that, bitching at myself all the while for giving in too easily.

But finally, I had to admit it to myself. I was actually relieved.

How many days could I have spent alone on my shack upon the sea?

Maybe a week. Maybe two. But then I would have gotten antsy, anxious for another mission.

So now I had one.

Too early, maybe.

But in the deepest part of me, I was glad. Because once you know the strange dark joy of a dangerous job, you can never be satisfied without it.

And I had been hooked long ago. Maybe even as a kid, working the trapeze in the circus; knowing that the slightest mistake could mean death. And once you have lived in the deadly glimmer of the razor's edge, everything else seems pallid in comparison.

The only thing that really bothered me was having to work with a stranger—one Lieutenant Santarun, an unknown factor. Fizer didn't know much about him—only that it was Santarun who had presented the theory that the three agents might have assassination in mind. Nothing concrete, Fizer had said. Just a hunch. But a hunch that had to be pursued. So I was to be the slightly stupid charterboat captain out to make a few quick bucks, and Santarun was to be a Cuban-American citizen in search of relatives.

Unless things got rough. Too rough for Santarun. And then—and only then—could I come from the safe cover of anonymity. For me, it meant leaving at home the obvious offensive weapons of the professional killer: the brutal AK-47 Russian assault rifle I had smuggled back from Nam, and the Navy-issue .45 of my SEAL days. But as a SEAL I had been trained to recognize the options, and make those options damned deadly. And aboard, I carried options enough.

At the fuel docks, it was the guy carrying the camera pack who first got me suspicious. As I said, he spent too much time watching me and not enough time looking through his viewfinder. Even so, he kept the lens of the remote unit trained on me— even while his partner, a stocky guy with the plastic grooming of an anchorman, seemed to be interviewing another charterboat captain fixing to leave for Mariel Harbor.

So I ignored it at first. Just pulled on my aviator Polaroids and tugged my old khaki fishing cap with

the long visor down over my ears while I finished
fueling. After all, the film-at-eleven newshounds
hadn't been exactly strangers in Key West lately. The
motels were full of them, all strutting up and down
Duval, wearing their press tags, looking bored and
officious and getting sloppy drunk on expense ac-
counts. The exodus of refugees from Mariel Harbor
had brought them on the run to Key West with the
same fervor of a shyster lawyer chasing an ambu-
lance. Blood is news. And news is money.

So I ignored them while I paid Harry at the docks
for my four hundred gallons of diesel, then throttled
Sniper on down to the cement wharves at the old
submarine base where I was to meet Fizer and pick
up Santarun.

And by the time I had thrown a couple of half
hitches around the big brass bollards, the two of
them were there again, pulling into the parking lot
in their rental Chevy. I watched the biggest one as
he put a fix on me from the corner of his eye while
the smaller one rounded up a couple of weary-
looking Cuban-American men to interview.

Same ploy.

The short, stocky one held the microphone in the
face of his "interviewee" while the remote unit swept
across me and *Sniper*.

It didn't make any sense. They had to have proper
press credentials or the guard wouldn't have let them
on the naval base. But why in the hell would anyone
want film of me?

I didn't like it. Not a bit. So I went below and

began stowing away the boxes of canned goods and
beer I had brought for the trip, giving them time to
make a move. Key West seems to get stranger and
stranger every year; an island that has become so
gaudily faddish, so populated with the weird and
undecipherable that you stop trying to find motive
in the actions of others. Overhead, I could hear the
chopping ignitions of a Coast Guard helicopter—
escorting in another load of refugees, probably. And
from the nearby docks where the immigration people
were processing the new arrivals came the frenzied,
heartfelt chant:

Libertad, libertad, LIBERTAD . . .

Through the starboard port I could see the refugees
standing in a long line across the docks, barefoot and
worn by their struggles to get out of Cuba, but smiling as they chanted in the heat of the afternoon sun.

I watched them, wondering all the while if
America would, indeed, become the land of liberty
for them. And as I wondered, I wished them well—
all but the Castro agents I knew stood among them;
those who had come to America seeking nothing but
the opportunity to destroy.

Back on the wide cement loading runway which
fronted Trumbo Annex, the two Cuban guys with the
television equipment were still at it. They moved
among the steady rush of the departing and the arriv-
ing, conspicuously staying within viewing distance of
me and *Sniper*—and equally as conspicuously trying
to pretend as if they weren't.

I climbed up on the wharf and began to amble

toward them. I still had about fifteen minutes before Fizer was supposed to arrive with Santarun, and I had decided to make the most of it. When the big guy with the gold chains and the vee of black chest thatch saw me coming, he immediately swerved the camera away, trying to ignore me. About ten feet from them I stopped, studied the sky, studied my worn Topsiders, a sham attempt to look inconspicuous, turning the tables on them. The stocky anchorman was interviewing an elderly man who, apparently, had just arrived. The exchange was in rapid Spanish. I don't know why, but people who speak Spanish seem to talk faster and louder than people who speak other languages.

So I had no problem hearing what they were saying, and, even with my bad Spanish, understanding what they were talking about.

Typical broadcast questions. And typical broadcast answers.

But that still didn't explain why they had been trying to get some film of me and my vessel.

But they would explain.

You could bet the bank on that.

The big guy with the gold chains was all attention now, focusing through the viewfinder, watching his squat companion work.

They knew I was only ten or fifteen feet away.

You're damn right they knew.

I watched them for a while, saying nothing, then my eyes caught the progress of an emaciated stray dog weaving along the docks. Too many stray dogs in Key West. The hippy kids and the drug lovers all come to Key West with a dog because they think the presence of a big pet suggests that they are sensitive, humane.

They're humane, all right—until the pet inconveniences them in some way, or they have a chance to go cruising. And then it's goodbye pet. They let the dogs loose then, ignoring the fact that stray dogs don't live long on a island teeming with heartworms, fast traffic, and crowded pounds.

This dog was some mixture of shepherd and collie; a fine, tall dog so skinny that his loose skin hung upon his ribs. He came angling across the wharf, tongue out, eyes glassy, then suddenly cut between the two Cubans—ruining, apparently, the camera shot.

"Oye! Perra . . . remara!"

The big guy with the camera pack gave the stray a solid kick in the stomach, tumbling it. The dog whimpered, got back up, and trotted off, not even bothering to look back. Its tongue was still out, its eyes still glassy.

I squatted down, and the dog came weaving toward me. It hesitated, then allowed me to scratch its ears, finally relaxing beneath my hands.

Tough life, hey partner?

He looked up into my eyes seeming to answer, then nudged my arm with his nose. It was wearing one of those cheap leather collars with no identification tag, and the collar was so tight that it had grown into the skin around the neck. I took out my Gerber belt knife, cut the collar, and pulled it gently away. The dog's tail thumped his gratitude. I looked over toward the two television guys.

"Hey!"

They pretended to ignore me. The old man was gone now, and the two of them stood shoulder to shoulder, conferring.

"Hey, you! *Cabrón!*"

The Spanish insult brought the big guy whirling around. He glared at me, then looked quickly away.

"How would you like someone to kick you in the stomach?"

The two of them pretended not to hear me, then moved toward the stairs of the old barracks on the wharf where the public restrooms are located. I watched them head up the steps, then quickly walked my starving friend back to *Sniper*, opened up two big cans of stew, and in another bowl put some water beside him on the dock.

I'll be back in a minute to see if you want dessert.

The dog stopped wolfing the food only long enough to watch me head for the old barracks.

The hundred-watt bulb which lighted the stairway was unshaded; and the halls of the deserted building were littered with trash and cigarette butts. There was anti-Castro graffiti on the walls, and someone with a belly full of yellow rice and beer hadn't quite made it to a suitable place to upchuck.

All compliments of the wave of humanity attracted by the Freedom Flotilla.

I moved quietly up the cement stairs, holding the railing, taking my time.

At the top of the stairs on the second floor I could hear muted Spanish coming from beyond the door of the public restroom. I put my ear to the door and listened, deciphering only bits and pieces of the conversation; a word here, and a word there. But then one word in particular caught my attention:

". . . MacMorgan . . ."

So they did know who I was.

And they had been following me.

I waited for a moment longer, listening, then pushed open the door. The shock on their faces was apparent, but immediately stifled by looks of contrived disinterest. I went ambling up to the biggest of them, smiling my best smile, trying to look small and friendly and harmless.

But I wasn't feeling harmless.

Maybe these two characters were the tail end of the CIA's security leak.

Maybe my identity as one of Stormin' Norman Fizer's troubleshooters was no secret after all.

The big guy with the gold chains had a sharp, angular face with black feral eyes and a mustache that had enjoyed a lifetime of vanity and expensive wax. The smaller one, the anchorman, stood behind him, his shoulder to me—afraid to ignore my entrance completely. He wore a burnt-orange blazer which said "TV 1" on the lapel.

"Geez," I said, "are you guys really gonna put my

picture on television?" I was still moving toward the big guy, the one who had kicked the dog.

"*No habla,*" he said.

But his eyes told me that he had understood.

"I saw you aiming that camera at me, and I just wanted to ask what time I'm gonna be on, 'cause I sure don't want to miss it."

"*No habla!*"

The big guy was still backing up, but he didn't look frightened. If anything, his face showed contempt.

The bright-blue news camera with its shoulder brace rested against the metal booth which contained the stool, and I stood between the camera and the two Cubans. The urinal was behind them, and the big guy looked as if he was tired of backing up anyway. He might have been an inch taller than me, but I had the weight.

And either way, it didn't matter.

Still bearing my stupid smile, I reached down deliberately and hefted the camera up with my left hand.

"This sure is some fancy setup."

"Get your hands off that!"

It was the big guy with the gold chains.

"Well, you sure do learn English fast," I said innocently. He took a step toward me, and I stopped him with a glare. I began to fiddle with the butterfly screws on the side of the camera, talking all the while. "You know when you two first pissed me off?"

They said nothing.

"You first pissed me off when you were filming me down at the fuel docks and didn't even have the courtesy to try and interview me first."

One of the butterfly screws went twisting across the floor.

"Hey, dammit, there's film in there!"

I cut the big guy off. "I mean, why would you two want my picture and no sound to go with it?"

"I don't know what your problem is, mister, but if you expose that film we're going to the police!"

I ignored him, still working on the second screw. "And do you know when you really pissed me off? It was when you kicked that poor stray dog. I just can't tell you how mad it makes me to see a grown man kick some poor defenseless animal.

"But do you know what your mistake was?" The final screw came off, and in one swift motion, I jerked the film cassette out, kicked the john door open, and tossed the film into the stool. "Your big mistake, *cabrón*, was that that dog wasn't defenseless. Because I've just appointed myself as his honorary bodyguard."

The big guy with the gold chains was better than I thought he'd be.

I expected him to shove me. Or take a big roundhouse swing at me.

That's what the inexperienced ones usually do. They're reluctant to fight, or they want to immediately go for a knockout like the hero of a western movie does it.

But this guy, obviously, was not what you would call inexperienced.

He faked a big right hand, and when I leaned away from it he drove his left foot up in a snapping upper-cut kick.

Luckily, I got most of it with my shoulder.

The anchorman acted like he wanted to get behind me—maybe just to escape, or maybe to try and get a crack at the back of my head.

I couldn't wait to find out. I cocked my left fist back, looking at the big cameraman all the while, then let the anchorman have a full—and completely unexpected—right to the solar plexus, that vulnerable center of nerve endings and tissue located below the soft veeing of the rib cage.

He went down with a loud *oomph*, kicking his legs wildly like a cartoon character overcome with laughter.

"What the hell is this all about?" The big guy's Spanish accent was much stronger with emotion now. He eyed his friend nervously, reluctant to take his attention completely off me. "It was just a goddam dog."

"Maybe. Maybe not. Why were you filming me?"

"I wasn't filming you."

I slapped him with forehand and backhand across the face, backing him up to the urinal. "Not polite to lie," I said evenly.

His face was red with slapping, and his forehead was white, leached of blood. "Okay," he said. "Okay. I'll tell you."

Waiting for him to explain, I relaxed. A stupid thing

to do. I was off guard just enough so that his next snapping kick caught me full in the kidney and sent me wheeling against the wall.

He was on me in a second, choosing to go with some nasty infighting. He was big and tough and strong. But not strong enough. You never want to wrestle shoulder to shoulder with someone who spent his boyhood working the double trapeze.

It's just not healthy.

I got my fingers wrapped around his biceps, squeezing, swinging him back and forth at will. In any fight there comes a moment—long before the fight has ended, usually—when one man realizes that he is overmatched and bound to lose.

In the ring, the victim of the sudden insight sets about not trying to win, but only to lose more slowly.

In a street fight, he tries to get the hell away.

And that's what the big cameraman tried now. He twisted away from me, took a long, lurching step toward the door, then came to an abrupt, ripping halt when I grabbed him by the back of his silk shirt.

My hands on his shoulders, I swung him around, nailed him full-fisted on the side of the neck, and he went backpedaling across the room, crashing into the urinal.

Water from the broken urinal was spraying everywhere. From outside, I could hear the forlorn blast of whistle signals and the moist *proppa-proppa-pop* of the Coast Guard choppers escorting in boatloads of refugees. In the strange clarity of the moment, it seemed as if I were back in Nam.

And that this is what I was meant to do.

Always.

The anchorman wasn't out. But he pretended to be when I bent over him and ripped his press credential tag off his blazer. I checked the big cameraman's pulse, then took his credentials, too.

I'd give them to Fizer and have them checked out.

"Thanks for the interview," I said as I opened the bathroom door. The anchorman was too scared to even pretend that he had not heard.

Back on the cement wharf, in the shadow of *Sniper*, the lean shepherd had finished the stew and was lapping down water in great gulps.

Feeling better?

The shepherd wagged its tail and went on lapping water.

I have a friend with a big house and fenced-in yard on Big Pine Key who says he needs a watchdog. Interested?

The tail swung harder, the dog's whole butt end moving. He stopped drinking and stared up at me, a new light in his eyes.

I'd keep you myself, but there's no place to crap on a stilthouse. Stay here while I go call the guy.

The shepherd turned back to the water as I walked to the payphone by the old barracks.

By the time I got back, Fizer was standing on the cement dock beside *Sniper*. He wore the obligatory business suit—this one an eggshell white.

"Very tropical," I said.

"The suit? Yeah, all I need is a big porch and a mint julep. You about ready?"

I nodded. "Where's Santarun?"

He checked his watch. "Should be here any minute." He had a funny look on his face. "Dusky, there's something I didn't know about the lieutenant that I have to tell you. . . ."

"Right," I said. "But before he gets here, I have to tell you about a little run-in I just had with a couple of television newsmen who I think are plants."

That caught his attention. So I told him the whole story and gave him their credentials.

He looked them over, then said, "I don't recognize the names, but I'll run them through the computers." He smiled wryly. "And if they turn out to be real newsmen, I'll come and visit when they jail you on assault charges."

"Right," I said. "Sure."

"Is that the dog?"

The shepherd had curled up on *Sniper's* aft deck. Its tail thumped lazily when Fizer motioned toward it.

"Yeah, and I'd appreciate it if you see that it gets to Big Pine Key."

I told him the address, and explained why.

Fizer eyed the shepherd. "Doesn't look like much of a watchdog to me."

"All it needs is something to protect. I doubt if he's ever had the chance."

At that moment, one of the Navy's blue Chevy

Nova staff cars came wheeling up and skidded to an abrupt halt. The driver got out, face aloof, somber.

"Wait a minute," I said. "That's not Santarun, is it?"

"That's what I was trying to tell you a moment ago. I didn't know. . . ."

The lieutenant lifted a sea bag and a suitcase from the car, slammed the trunk, then came walking toward *Sniper*: dark; long-legged walk; a haughty figure in jeans and black T-shirt that offered nothing but challenge.

Lieutenant Santarun was one of the most beautiful women I had ever seen in my life. . . .

5

She was one of the aloof ones. It's all too common among the truly beautiful females. Maybe they have to be—I don't know. Maybe it's some kind of emotional fence to keep out the mass of adoring males. Or maybe it really is a form of conceit. Whatever it was, this Lieutenant Santarun had a ton of it. Norm made the introductions. He kept it businesslike, playing his part: he didn't know me; I was just a charterboat bum hired to take this woman to Mariel Harbor.

"Captain MacMorgan—Dusky, was it?"

I nodded.

He motioned toward Lieutenant Santarun. "This is Androsa Santarun, my client. As I told you, Ms. Santarun's father is still living in Cuba. Your job is to see that she gets to Mariel Harbor safely and picks up her father, then see that they both make it back safely."

"No problem," I said. "It shouldn't take us more than—"

"Mr. Fizer," she interrupted. It was a flat, corporate voice with only the slightest trace of an accent. "Did you apprise Mr. MacMorgan of who will have the final decision-making responsibility in regard to anything which concerns this trip?"

Norm almost stammered. "Well, I was just about to . . ."

She turned to me. Her hair was a lustrous blue-black, piled severely atop her head. It served only to accentuate the fine feminine lines of her face, the smooth, clear olive skin, and her piercing mahogany eyes. There was something tough about those eyes. Something tough and challenging—oddly incongruous with the lithe, ripe contours plainly outlined by jeans and black T-shirt. Her breasts were small but well formed. Her legs were long, tapering from thighs to hips with only a curved implication of pelvic hinge. There was a proper narrowing of waist, and the sensual impact of womanhood where jeans and plain brown belt converged. I had to force my eyes back to meet hers.

"The boat is mine, ma'am," I said, hating myself for having to show deference to anyone—male or female—who would presume to take control of *Sniper.* "I make the decisions when it comes to my boat."

Her eyes widened ever so slightly, and she moved a fraction of a step closer to me. "Mr. MacMorgan, it may be your boat but it's my charter. I think it

wise before we even get started to establish what
your role will be. You are being paid and paid well
for this trip. And I don't think it unreasonable to
demand that I have control over matters concerning
it—"

"As long as it doesn't endanger the boat," Norm
added quickly. He looked at me in the level manner
of a lawyer trying to protect his client. "I'm afraid
that's the deal, Captain MacMorgan. Are you still
interested?"

I thought about it for a moment, cursing myself
silently for ever letting myself get involved. In the
fishing guide business, you get a bellyful of unpleas-
ant strangers aboard the boat you treasure. The good
ones are a joy—but the ones like this Santarun, the
haughty ones are nothing but a big pain in the ass.
No, I wasn't still interested. But I had committed
myself. Was I such a ridiculous male chauvinist animal that I would balk at being under the command
of a woman? Not normally. But aloofness and arro-
gance in men or women are nothing more than
symptoms of some deeper character flaw—and that's
exactly why I liked to work alone. Goddammit, I
have enough problems of my own to have to worry
about the potentially deadly shortcomings of others.

But I had no choice. Not if I didn't want to let
Norm down.

"Yeah," I said. "I'm still interested." I shot Norm
a few private darts with my eyes, checked my watch
and added, "Get your stuff aboard, ma'am. We can
be in Mariel Harbor before midnight if we hurry."

I turned back to my boat and left them both standing there on the dock, feeling—imagining, at least—Lieutenant Androsa Santarun's irritation because I hadn't carried her bags.

It's funny how, when you are leaving for a strange land, even the well-known surroundings you travel seem to take on a quality of that strangeness. I steered from the flybridge, getting as far away from the woman as I could. Behind me, the piles of rock below old Fort Taylor, the green haze of Australian pine on the beach to the east, the squat, dun-colored fort itself, and the checkered water tower—all of which I knew so well—suddenly appeared eerily unfamiliar. It was a rolling, turquoise afternoon at sea when we left. Wind was out of the southeast, seven to ten knots, giving us a fine quartering sea. I picked up the range markers a few miles off, then the nun buoy at East Triangle reef, and headed out Mainship Channel, Cuba-bound.

Cuba-bound.

I sat back on the big pilot's chair, seeing nothing but sea for miles around. The water changed from milky green to clear jade—the spoil area off East Triangle looking shallow, dark, and dangerous. And when we were finally clear of markers, and the water was purple-black with no bottom, I guessed the strength of the Gulf Stream at about four knots, and adjusted my course to 225 degrees, then switched her temporarily to automatic pilot.

I climbed down the ladder and went through the hatch into the salon.

Androsa Santarun was at the little booth, and when I entered she quickly covered up something she had been reading. I knew it wasn't mine. The few things I had that I didn't want anyone to see were hidden in the forward bilge compartment, under the indoor-outdoor carpet.

"You could have knocked," she said tersely.

"Don't see why."

"I might have been dressing!"

"It's okay, ma'am—I have a little sister," I said, already sorry for having indulged myself in that kind of silly remark. Beautiful or not, the fact that her breasts were not large must have, at some point in her life, concerned her. It was a cheap shot, and I knew it, so I just knelt by the little refrigerator, put three beers in a paper sack to keep them cold, then headed back out the door without saying another word.

"I suppose you'll go up there and get drunk now." She had recovered her composure, but her face was still flushed. "Isn't that what fishing guides do?"

"Ma'am, if I wanted to get drunk, I'd carry the refrigerator above and leave this sack of beer below—to cure the hangover."

"Mr. MacMorgan, if we are to get along on this trip, I suggest you curb your wisecracks." Her face was strained, deadly serious.

I took a breath, exhaled, then caught her mahogany

eyes with mine. Within them, for the briefest of moments, I saw the gray light of some undecipherable desperation—then nothing else. They turned flat again . . . wooden. It was concession time—and I had the feeling it would be the first of many. For me.

"You're right, Miss Santarun. I'm sorry."

Back above on the flybridge, it felt good to be away from the intensity of her. It was more than just the intensity of a woman compelled to dominate. And it was more than sexuality—although sexuality was like an aura of dark heat which surrounded her. She was one of the ageless ones, anywhere between twenty-eight and thirty-eight; one of the eternal female animals who, in eons past, would have had men in bearskins traveling from miles around to fight for her with clubs and teeth. But the intensity originated from something else. I couldn't put my finger on it.

So I decided not to waste my time.

It was a mission. Nothing more. Nothing less. I would take her to Mariel, and if Castro's goons swiped her, fine. It was a chance that was hers to take. And if they didn't take her, and we ended up hauling back General Halcón—who I assumed would pose as Santarun's father—then that would be fine too.

I would go into it with my eyes open. But I would follow orders, goddammit.

Just like in Nam.

It was a good day for the crossing. Just enough sea to lift, roll, then drop the boat back into the turquoise troughs. It was a quartering port breeze that carried *Sniper*'s diesel exhaust fumes on back to Key West, and golden sargassum weed lay before me in the black iridescence of deep sea.

Cuba-bound.

Sitting on the flybridge, wind in my face, I tried to remember the way it had been on my first trip to Havana.

What had I been? Fourteen? Maybe.

Papa had set it up. Arranged to have me and the Italian trapeze family that had adopted me brought over on the ferry which left Key West from where the Pier House is today. We did one show outside the Hotel Nacional and another at the Tropicana Club, where the girls wore gaudy costumes of imitation satin and fruit-basket hats, and where, outside, the ficus trees draped over and kept the sidewalks so slippery that Papa's only advice to us was, "Take care you don't fall on your asses going in."

It was good advice.

The Cubans loved Papa, for his books had already been translated into Spanish. We were circus stars accompanied by a star of greater magnitude—but no one cared. Least of all me. Because the Cubans treated us better for his sponsorship. And in the '50s, there was no place better to have fun than Havana— even for a kid.

So I wondered about Cuba; wondered how it had changed. I had been back twice since that first trip. Once I went for the fishing off the Isla de Pinos— and it was great. The most recent trip wasn't so ter-

rific. Strictly business. And we were never given opportunity enough to make it anything other than a
failure.

So that's what I thought about as I steered *Sniper*
over the green wash of sea, toward the empty horizon. I cracked open the second cold beer, retrieved
the circular tin of Copenhagen from my blue salt-
bleached shirt, and felt the pleasant burn of tobacco
against my lip.

The woman could stay below for the entire trip as
far as I was concerned.

To hell with her. The sea spread out jadelike, swollen and singular beneath May sky, and that was
enough. I wasn't going to allow her the high price
of concern.

To hell with all the narrow, self-obsessed jerks,
male and female, who spoil the scenery with their
flatulent personalities. I raised the bottle of beer in a
half-mast toast—and that's when I noticed it.

A partially submerged cruiser well off to port,
locked in place by the conflict of foul wind and foul
Stream current.

The reflection of sunlight on glass had caught my
attention. I banked east, opened throttles to three-
quarters, and bore down on the boat.

As I drew closer, I could see that it was more
trawler than cruiser. And the trawler was not alone.
A Mako center-console, twenty to twenty-five feet
long, with its sweep of gunwales tapering toward the
stern, had rafted up beside it.

From behind me, I heard the woman's voice. She

had, apparently, felt the sudden change of course and had come topside to see what was going on.

"I think there's a boat in trouble up there, Miss Santarun. I'm going to have a look."

"But isn't that another boat with it? Aren't they already helping?"

She stood beside me, wind pulling at the pile of black hair as we powered on to thirty knots. I could smell the closeness of her: a frail odor of soap and some kind of body powder.

"Maybe it is, maybe it isn't."

"But why else would another boat—"

"It won't take long, ma'am. Besides, it's against the law for me not to offer assistance."

She hesitated for a moment, then climbed back down the ladder. I wasn't exactly unhappy to see her leave.

I was downwind of them, so I was within fifty yards of the boats before I throttled down. The trawler had listed to starboard, bow high, aft deck partially submerged. It rolled in the weak wave crest like a disabled animal. The trawler was white fiberglass with red trim, and a good bit larger than my own *Sniper*, which is a little smaller—but a hell of a lot faster—than most sportfishermen. The skiff lashed up beside it was a Mako 23 with twin Johnson 200s. The name on the side of the Mako was factory-painted, blue letters two feet high: *Talon*. I could see only one man aboard the Mako. He seemed preoccupied with something on the deck.

"Do you need any assistance?"

The man looked up, startled. He was a black man, thin and angular in a loose white shirt. He rode with the roll of waves momentarily, staring at me.

"I said, 'Do you need some assistance?' "

He shook his head and yelled back at me, "Naw, man. Just called the Coast Guard. Best stay back—this boat here's about to go down!"

There was something about him I didn't like. He seemed nervous, uncommunicative. At open sea the vastness, the loneliness, normally affects people just the opposite—they become talkative, unfailingly polite.

But not this guy.

"I've been listening to VHF all afternoon, and I didn't hear any call—maybe your radio's busted."

It was a lie. I hadn't listened to VHF after the first hour. The steady chain of distress calls, and the endless question from Key West Coast Guard—*"Do you have any refugees aboard?"*—had caused me to switch it off in minor protest.

But I wanted to test him. I wanted to see his reaction.

He thought for a moment, shrugged.

"I'll call them for you right now!"

He fidgeted now, uneasiness intensifying. And I had him figured.

There was probably another guy with him—belowdeck in the disabled trawler. And they hadn't stopped to give aid.

They were pirates.

That simple.

In three hundred years, nothing has really changed off the Florida Keys. People come and go, but the pirates—generation after generation—stay. The trawler had probably been a victim of the deadly squall. And this guy had come out looking for floaters: boats to strip, unattended vessels to plunder.

And after that storm, there would be plenty to find.

I edged *Sniper* closer, wishing to hell I'd brought a weapon. I could have thrown it overboard before reaching Mariel Harbor. But I hadn't, so I kept my eye on the guy as I approached, never wavering.

"Boat's 'bout to go down, man! Better stay back!"

Sure.

Had he really believed the trawler was about to sink, he'd have dumped the line to which the Mako was connected.

And as I got closer, I could see what had preoccupied him. On the deck of the skiff was a mound of ship's stores and supplies, only partially covered by a red tarp. He saw my look, the contempt on my face.

It was a stupid move on my part. No doubt about it. You can end up very dead when you let emotion reign over good sense. I should have backed off then and there and radioed the Coast Guard. But when you work around boats you come to despise those who leech their living from the misfortunes of others. Maybe the people who had been on the trawler were struggling in a life raft close by. But you could bet that bastard hadn't—and wouldn't—notify anybody about finding a disabled vessel.

So I moved on in.

"Did you have to kill anybody to get that crap—or did you just find 'em dead and throw them overboard?"

"Now, wait a minute there, man—"

"I don't feel like waiting a minute, buddy. Just answer me. Was there anybody aboard when you got here?"

He gave me a strange smile, then. A strange lethal smile—the kind you sometimes see on cats hidden beside a bird feeder. It didn't look like he was armed. But I was wrong. The back of his pants had been covered by the tail of the loose shirt. And that's exactly where he began to move his hand. I knew what he had in mind. Kill me, toss me into the depths of the Stream, then plunder my boat, too.

By the time he was bringing the little snubnosed revolver up out of his back-mounted holster, I knew exactly what I had to try to do. The bowrail of *Sniper* threw its shadow across the stern of the Mako—that's how close I had gotten. His back was against the low gunwale of the stern quarter, and before him was the red tarp and the mound of stolen ship's supplies. Chances were good that even at that close range he would have missed me with the snubnose.

But I had taken enough chances.

As his right hand lifted the revolver, his left hand came down like a clamp to steady his right wrist, taking aim. And as he did, I turned the wheel full to starboard, punched the port engine full-bore, and jumped to plane in an explosion of diesel exhaust and water. It was a long, tricky moment as I swung immediately back to port—making sure I didn't nail the Mako with my stern. And when I looked back, ducking, to check the clearance, I saw the unexpected. I had hoped the black guy with the gun would go toppling overboard backward with the force of my wake. Instead, he lay on his side on the deck of the skiff, clawing in dreadful slow motion at a strange reddish ember which had suddenly appeared on his cheek, just below his left eye.

And then the ember began to spurt blood.

He crawled shakily to his knees, touching his cheek with a hand.

He had a look of puzzlement on his face. He looked at the blood on his hand, cocked his head wryly and looked at me.

And then he fell dead on the mound of plunder in front of him, his blood darker than the scarlet of the tarp.

Sniper was back to dead idle now. I paused for a thoughtful moment trying to figure out just what in hell had happened.

And then I knew.

I looked back toward the fighting deck, and there was the woman, Androsa Santarun. She had used the angle of the VHF antenna and teak gunwale as a brace—the lithe shape of her hidden by the extension of the salon wall. The .38 she held in her left hand was still poised, ready.

6

The only emotion she showed as she punched the empty cartridge overboard into the depthless sea was anger.

Anger at me.

There was no remorse, no feminine hysterics at what she had just done. The Mako still rolled in the dissipating wake of *Sniper*, and the dead man's head weaved back and forth in the wash and draw of it. I clunked my engines into reverse, backing off a way so we would not drift down into the trawler, then started to climb down to the fighting deck.

"And just what do you think you're doing, Mr. MacMorgan?"

She was mad, all right. She bit the words off, the low alto of her voice a pitch higher.

Truthfully, I didn't know why I was climbing down to her. I had the vague idea she might faint or burst into tears . . . or something. When I hit the deck, I turned to her. Oddly, she seemed somehow smaller with a gun in her hand; a whole head shorter than me, more than a hundred pounds lighter. I stood looking down into her perfect face and realized exactly what had made her seem taller, fuller: the impact of her; the intensity of beauty, sexuality, and those mahogany eyes. Now, mad as she was—and even holding the gun—she looked almost frail.

But not vulnerable.

No way. Not the way she handled a weapon.

"Maybe I wanted to thank you for saving my life," I said.

"Mr. MacMorgan, I truthfully don't give a damn about your life. All I wanted to save was my . . . my *trip*. I told you not to come over here. But you insisted . . ."

Her anger added flavor to her faint Spanish accent, softening the A's, blurring her R's.

"Not a matter of insisting. It was my decision."

"Damn your decisions!"

She was mad, all right. For a moment, I thought she was going to take a swing at me. And I had to choke back the grin I felt fighting its way to the surface.

"Fine," I said. "My decisions be damned. But now we're going over and have a look at that trawler. There might be someone else aboard." There was something else I had to say—say to protect my own cover, if nothing else. So I did. "By the way, where did you learn how to use a handgun like that?"

I watched her closely for a reaction, but there was none.

"All you have to do, Mr. MacMorgan, is run the boat. What I know and what I do is none of your concern. And if you ever do anything this stupid again, I'll . . . I'll . . ."

I couldn't help it then. I felt the silly grin take my face.

"You'll what—shoot me too?"

She had quite a left. Her nostrils flared, her eyes became slits, and she threw a big roundhouse at my chin. It was to be no open-handed slap, either. The pretty brown fingers were clenched into a fist. I leaned away from it, caught her small hand in the palm of my left, and squeezed gently. I saw her teeth clench into a grimace. I lightened my grip and said evenly, "Woman, you'd be well advised never to try that again."

I dropped her hand, turned, and climbed back up to the flybridge, hearing her stalk off below.

I nudged *Sniper* up to the trawler. The stern was almost completely submerged, waves rolling over the transom. But the cleat on the port side of the transom was still above water, so I got a line around it, careful to pass it through by bow chock before securing it with a temporary slippery hitch. I left *Sniper*'s engines gurgling—in case I wanted to back off quickly.

And just as I was about to step over onto the trawler, the woman came up behind me.

She said, "Don't you think the person with the gun should go first?"

I looked at her. She was calmer now, some of the anger gone. She held the revolver in her left hand.

"You're right," I said. "I'll carry it with me."

She shook her head. "No. That's not what I meant. I'll go first."

"I thought you wanted to get to Mariel Harbor safely."

It was as close as she had come all day to smiling. "That's exactly why I don't want you stumbling around with a loaded gun in your hand."

I stepped back and made a grandiose sweeping gesture with my arm. "After you, Miss Santarun."

Using the line for balance, she jumped lithely to the transom of the trawler, then walked knee deep in water toward the wheelhouse. It's eerie boarding any abandoned boat at open sea, but an abandoned boat that is hopelessly sinking adds a touch of the macabre which makes you strain to listen and obligates you to whisper. The ropes creaked in the wash of ocean, and a halyard *tap . . . tap-tap-tapped* in the light wind.

I expected the dead man's partner to be hidden somewhere in the cabin of the trawler. And I didn't want the woman to face him alone. So by the time she was entering the wheelhouse, I was right behind her, Gerber skinning knife in hand.

Even in the bright May sunlight, it seemed dark inside. Water covered the floor, and cushions and charts and clothing floated in shallow chaos. The electronic equipment had been ripped out by the dead pirate, and a box of more plunder—Danforth compass, ship's bell, and a life ring, face down— sat on the booth table, waiting to be loaded onto the Mako.

"Why don't you let me have the handgun and go first?"

Androsa Santarun held up her hand, telling me to be quiet. She stepped into the water of the wheel-house, the revolver following along with the sweep of her eyes. She pulled open a storage closet, then tried a cabin light—which didn't work.

"It doesn't seem likely he'd be by himself."

She shook her head, agreeing. "No," she said. "It doesn't."

On both sides of the wheelhouse were couches, the tops of which opened for storage. She lifted the first, then dropped it back.

Nothing.

I was about to check the other one—but that's when I noticed. A line of bullet holes riveted inward along the port wall.

She saw them, too.

"Automatic weapon," I said. And then I added quickly in reply to her quizzical look, "I was in Nam for a year. You learn all about automatic weapons in the Army."

The holes swept across the bulkhead in a long arc, the smashed windows of the wheelhouse evidence of where they had finally halted.

"The guy in the Mako didn't have a weapon like

that. If he had, he'd have used it on me long before you got your shot off."

"Possibly," she said. "But who else would want to shoot at some innocent private boat?"

"Drug runners," I said. "It's not all that unusual. Maybe the people running this boat were carrying a load and the competition caught up with them. Or maybe they were just out here fishing and saw something they weren't supposed to see. Like I said— it happens."

She sighed. "I guess you'd better notify the Coast Guard—"

She stopped then, listening intently.

"Did you hear that—*shush*."

She tilted her head, straining to listen. And then I heard it, too. A soft, rhythmic *thunk . . . thunk*, coming from the forward berth beyond the door.

"Give me the revolver."

She looked at me, said nothing, then headed for the door, the .38 poised.

She put her right hand on the doorknob, hesitated for a moment, then jerked it open.

The water was deeper in the forward cabin. It came out in a black wash, calf-deep, rivering more floating junk—and something else, too.

A man, face up.

He was naked to the waist, his arms thrown out as if caught in some strange slow-motion fall.

His hair was short, blacker than the water, and his hands and face were a ghastly white.

He looked as if he was in his mid-twenties. A gray blotch marked where his wristwatch had been. The mustache on his face looked ridiculously neat in comparison to the rest of his drained flesh.

His throat had been cut; cut so deeply that his head bobbed slowly in the water as if it were about to come off. And that's why the water was black—black with his blood.

The woman was stock-still at first. Then she covered her mouth suddenly and stumbled toward me. I locked my arm around her, feeling ribs heave beneath breasts, holding her close.

"Oh my God," she said. "Oh my God. . . ."

It was what the reporters would probably call an appalling sight.

And they would have been right. His face was contorted, locked in the horror of his final conflict: teeth bared, eyes wide, wolflike. Quickly, I moved the woman away from the body, over by the built-in couch.

"It's awful," she said. Her hands still covered her mouth.

"Feel like you're going to be sick?"

She shook her head and braced one elbow on the box of ship's hardware that had never quite made it to the Mako. "No," she said. "I'll be okay. Just give me a second."

With my foot, I rolled the corpse over. It was already bloated, spongy.

I was looking for a bullet wound, but found none.

It didn't make sense. Why had the black man slit the throat of his own partner?

Or maybe it wasn't his partner. Maybe it was the guy who had owned the boat. And maybe some drug runners had gotten to him first. . . .

I opened the narrow compartment below the wheel where the ship's papers should have been kept.

Empty.

Somebody had beat me to them.

I decided to check the skiff.

I took the woman gently by the arm. "We've got to get out of here," I said. "This boat isn't going to last much longer. One good wave and she'll turn turtle."

She seemed to be still in a daze. Shooting the pirate hadn't seemed to bother her. But the way this guy died, it even made me a little queasy myself.

"Let's go," I said again. "We'll cut the Mako loose and call the Coast Guard—"

The moment I said it, the couch seat I had not gotten around to checking came flying off. It knocked me back against the wall and, in slow-motion realization, I knew what was happening. The pirate's partner was hiding in there, hoping to hell we'd just leave. But I had forced his hand—said I wanted to free the Mako, his only means of escape from this sinking boat.

I didn't see him or his pistol, but I heard the first shot—and saw the woman drop to a heap on the water-slick floor.

"Hold it right there, or I'll kill you, too!"

High voice, on the edge of hysterics. It was a kid. Not much older than twenty. Blond hair, tan face with a sneer that showed a row of bad teeth. When your life is on the line, you don't take time to reason. The instincts take over and the brain digests visual information at near superhuman speed all in a glance: Androsa Santarun was not dead—slightest movement of chest, no blood; the kid wasn't comfortable with a weapon—held it awkwardly, like a snake; whether I halted or not, the kid would kill us both. He had to.

I tossed the couch seat at him and dove for his feet, hearing, as I dove, the pistol explode and the crash of window glass. I jerked his feet out from under him and tried to smother his arms.

Didn't do a very good job. He got another shot off, right by my face. It made my ears ring and my head roar. But it missed.

"Watch out!"

It was the woman, on her feet again. There was a thin trickle of blood down her left cheek. She had recovered her .38 and had it leveled at the kid's head.

"What the hell are you doing?"

I saw her pull back the hammer, a strange, starry look in her eyes. But before she had a chance to fire, I hit the kid's blanched face with a heavy overhand right, knocking him cold.

I stood up, pointing at him. "There you go—an easy shot. Go ahead and shoot if you want to kill someone else so bad!"

She lowered the handgun slowly, trembling.

"I'm sorry," she said. "I just . . . just . . ."

I took her by the arm and steered her back out onto the deck.

"Do you know how to use a radio?"

She nodded.

"Good. I'm going to tie up the kid and stick him and the other guy in the Mako. You call the Coast Guard. Don't give my call letters. Just tell them there's a vessel in trouble. The Loran is beside the radio. Just tell them the numbers you see flashing. They'll understand. Got it?"

She shook her head stoically. "And then what?"

"And then I'm taking you back to Key West—"

"No!"

"We have to have someone look at your cheek."

She touched her face, then studied the blood on her hand, as if she had forgotten the wound. "He didn't shoot me—I hit my head when I dove to the floor, dammit! No, don't say another word. We're going on to the Mariel Harbor—that's the agreement!"

There was something almost pathetic about her fierceness. She looked like a Spanish version of one of television's Angels, determined as hell to solve the obligatory "mystery," fake blood and all.

But there was nothing fake about this woman—blood or mission or anything else.

"Okay," I said. "Fine. But when we get back, you do the explaining to the authorities."

Her firmness was edged with contempt. "Don't worry, Mr. MacMorgan. I'll see that you don't lose your precious boat."

She turned then, back toward *Sniper*. But before she did, she cast one more look into the wheelhouse of the trawler, at the dead man, at the kid—and at something else, too. The life ring. It had been knocked out of the box during the fight, and now floated right-side up in the shallow blood and water on the cabin floor. It explained the new determination in her. I knew the name from my conversation with Norm Fizer.

In black block letters, the life ring boasted the name of the trawler which now sank beneath us:

Storm Nest.

7

The first thing you raise approaching Cuba from open sea is a low bank of cumulus clouds appearing, on the curve of horizon, like a sudden Dakota windscape. The sea is a mile deep, purple-black in shafts of clear light, and flying fish lift in coveys before you, skimming cresting waves and luminous sargassum weed like locusts.

It was dawn.

Clouds were fire-laced to the southeast, and, later, the bleak facades of factories and pre-Castro highrise hotels below Havana caught the light in a blaze of geometrics. Mariel Harbor, already demarcation point for more than sixty thousand refugees, was just twenty miles to the west, a surge of dark cliffs.

The Coast Guard had held us up.

The Coasties and Norm Fizer.

Androsa had insisted on notifying her "lawyer" on VHF. I thought it a stupid move on her part—even though she played her role perfectly on the radio, telling Norm she might need "legal counsel" upon her return to Key West. She made no mention of the trawler's name. But still, there was no way of knowing if the Cubans were monitoring the Key West marine operator. And if there was a security leak in some high federal office, it wouldn't take long to realize who Fizer really was.

But I couldn't stop her without tipping my hand, so I said nothing.

We stood by aboard *Sniper*, waiting.

Fizer was on the first Coast Guard chopper out. A small cutter came later, and they sent a watch with pumps to try to save *Storm Nest*. While the Coasties worked, Norm came aboard *Sniper*. He was as businesslike as ever, but the good humor which I'd always known to dominate his personality was nowhere in sight.

He was damn concerned.

And I didn't blame him.

When he got into the salon, sat down with coffee and his briefcase, the woman looked at me irritably.

"Would you mind leaving us alone for a few minutes, Mr. MacMorgan."

From the corner of my eye, I saw Norm nod ever so slightly.

"No problem," I said. I went above to the flybridge and watched the Coast Guard work. Private boaters in the Keys tend to regard the Coasties as one big pain in the ass. And those that do have reasons—although not very good reasons. When the island isn't wild hauling refugees, the Coast Guard's biggest job is trying to stop the massive flow of drug traffic. It's an impossible job, of course, and they probably nab less than ten percent of the grass, coke, and heroin that comes into Florida. But they're a damn sight more competent than any other branch of the Department of Transportation, and they give it their best shot. And that means stopping and searching a lot of boats, innocent and otherwise. So the innocent boaters who get stopped react, inevitably, like outraged private citizens. They scream and squawk about their legal rights being violated, and demand to know why the Coast Guard doesn't need a warrant to board their vessel. And that just shows them to be the fools they are—ignorant of maritime law and, probably, all other Rules of the Road that that simple ignorance implies.

Of course, they're the first to condemn the Coast Guard or incompetence when they read in the papers about increased drug use in grade schools.

And they're the first to radio for help when their lack of seamanship gets them into big trouble.

So I watched the Coasties work with nothing short of admiration. The sea can be one hell of a desolate place, and I, for one, was glad to have them around.

While one watch worked at resurfacing *Storm Nest*, the cutter sent another crew in an old whaling-style boat to take care of the kid I had punched, and the two corpses. I watched their faces and saw them react to the horror of the man who had had his throat cut.

The face of death isn't all that unusual in their jobs. But I could tell they hadn't seen anything like that.

After an hour or so, Norm came climbing up to the flybridge. I looked behind him to see if Santarun was coming too.

He saw my glance, shook his head, and said, "She's down in the head. I'm supposed to be up here to offer you more money to continue on to Mariel."

"What?"

Norm shrugged. "She said you were trying to talk her into going back to Key West."

"Yeah. I was." I glanced below to make sure she couldn't hear me. "If she's one of the CIA's best people, it's no wonder that this country is having trouble in other parts of the world."

"I know, I know," he said wearily. "That was a stupid goddam move, notifying me by radio. The Coast Guard has orders to keep me *and* the CIA abreast of what's going on out here. But I guess she was so shocked to find *Storm Nest* back in American waters that she felt it was a necessary risk."

I looked over to where the Coast Guard had its big diesel pumps belching water out of the trawler. For the first time I could see part of its name on the stern. They were doing a good job.

"What do you figure happened to those three agents?"

"God knows. I spoke with Santarun about the guy whose throat had been cut. She says she's sure he's not one of the agents—and she knew them all pretty well. But I'm going to have a fingerprint expert check it out just to make sure."

"So if they did make it to Mariel Harbor and were kidnapped—or just disappeared on their own—who brought *Storm Nest* back to our waters?"

Norm thought for a moment, rubbing his jaw absently. "Well, how about this for one workable scenario: Our agents make it to Cuba, signal us that they're there, then disappear—never mind how or why. The Cubans, naturally, confiscate the trawler. Now there are plenty of soldiers, government employees, whatever, over there just looking for an opportunity to make a break for it. They can't have themselves declared refugees, because that would brand them as traitors and Castro would have them executed. So let's say the guy who got his throat cut was a soldier. He saw the confiscated trawler, decided it was plenty of boat to make the crossing and, when the time was right, he made a break for it. One of the Cuban gunboats shot the boat up some in the process, but he made it to international waters okay."

"So far so good," I said. "But then what?"

"Any number of things could have happened. But most probably he got boarded by drug runners, or maybe those two boat hunters in the Mako and"— he made a slicing motion with finger against throat— "they did him in."

"Chamber of commerce wouldn't like that explanation. The Florida Keys are supposed to be the friendliest islands under the sun."

Fizer grinned. "I won't tell anybody if you won't."

"So now what?"

Norm looked surprised. "Why, you go on to Mariel Harbor, that's what. We got one hell of a lucky break, you finding *Storm Nest* before she went down. Now we have to take advantage of it. You have to go over there and find out what in the hell's going on."

"I wouldn't mind that at all—if you agreed to take Santarun back to Key West with you."

"No way, Dusky. Absolutely not. She's the bait, and you're our ace in the hole."

"Norm, she's a pain in the ass! And she's erratic, too—and you know how dangerous that is."

"Wait a minute, MacMorgan." He hunched over in his seat, face close to mine. No way I could miss that wry look in his eyes. "The way she tells it, she saved your life back there—"

"Yeah, that's true—"

"So tell me how that's erratic. A waste of energy, maybe—but certainly not erratic."

"Norm," I said, "she killed that guy like she's been killing men all her life. But the next minute, she's about to wilt because some guy got his throat cut. A second later, she's screaming at me to move out of the way so she can blow some kid's head off. Now that's not exactly normal."

Fizer just sat there grinning. "You know what your problem is, MacMorgan?"

"Why spoil your fun? You're going to tell me anyway."

"That woman doesn't like you. She told me that.

She says you're stupid and a smart-ass and a little too bullheaded for your own good. And you just can't stand the idea of any beautiful woman not going all a-flutter over your boyish charm—especially a woman who is giving you orders."

Stormin' Norman Fizer stood up, signifying—if there was any doubt in my mind—that the discussion was over. He sniffed the wind and said, "Boy, I don't see how you can stand it out here. Too much clean air." He winked at me. "Now Washington's the place to live. Plenty of gas fumes to build your character. And there's always that poor fool in the White House to watch if there's nothing good on TV." He stopped in the middle of this discourse, looked at me seriously for a moment, then said, "Dusky, all I'm asking is that you put up with her until this thing is over. It's important. It really is. Telling a big ugly bastard like you this is kind of embarrassing, but it's true—you're the best man I have. Bar none. And I'm counting on you."

"Fizer," I said.

"Yeah, Dusky?"

"You're full of shit—you know that, don't you?"

He chuckled. "Yeah, I know that. It's one of the many things we have in common. . . ."

So it was to be a long night of black heavy sea, starlight on the southern horizon, and the frail bobbing glimmer of running lights in the distance.

Sniper pushed its way through the darkness with resolve—and the sweet sync of twin diesel engines.

I piloted from the main cabin. The woman slept below in the big forward vee-berth. Her conversation with Norm seemed to have steadied her. She was in control again: aloof and uncommunicative. It seemed perfectly natural to her that I should be the one to initiate supper. Cook it. Serve it. And wash the dishes.

So I did.

If there's one thing I learned about any outing with any other human being, it's this: Do more than your share of the monotonous chores, and don't worry about what your companion does or doesn't do. Because getting mad is worse than the chores themselves.

So, I opened two cans of stew, chopped in onion, added garlic, some of that good A&B hot sauce, and served it up with hot rolls.

"What is this stuff?" she had said when I shoved the tin plate across the galley table.

"What's it look like?"

"Nothing in particular."

"Then that's what it is."

"What about coffee?"

I nodded toward the dented gallon drip pot in its holder above the alcohol stove. "Good idea. I'll need a bunch of it tonight. Coffee's in the locker beneath the sink. I like it strong."

I took my dinner above to the full controls of the main cabin. While I ate, I switched on the red overhead chart light and checked our position with the 707 digital readout Loran C. The Stream was pushing me a little farther north and east than I thought it would, so I disengaged the little Benmar autopilot, adjusted our course, then clicked the dial, letting the soft hydraulic *whirr* take control of *Sniper*. Then I had sniffed the wind: smelled the dark scent of diesel, of wet rope, fiberglass, of bottom paint, and the good ozone smell of distant lightning blowing across open sea.

But no coffee.

So when I heard the woman finish brushing her teeth and head toward the forward berth, I went below, lit the stove and set coffee to boiling myself. And when the odor filled the boat, sharp and full and strong as whiskey, I poured myself a mug, added honey, and allowed myself the after-dinner luxury of fresh chew of Red Man, spitting over the side.

Busy night in the Florida Strait.

Busiest night in history, probably.

A quarter mile away, I heard the *choppa-choppa* roar of helicopter above the sound of waves and engines, and I turned to watch as the pilot of the chopper swept the sea with its brilliant spotlight, searching for something.

The night sea was green beneath the helicopter, as if illuminated by a lance of meteor, and then I saw the little skiff, running without lights, pounding through the quartering sea and heavily overloaded with refugees.

The helicopter pilot tried to contact the captain of the little skiff on VHF 16, giving his own call letters—

". . . Whiskey, Bravo, Alpha . . ."—but received no answer.

Obviously, the skiff had no radio.

"Stupid bastard," I said to myself. "The stupid, brave, bastard . . ."

No running lights. No radio. And a boat that was built for skiing on inland lakes—not the deadly Gulf Stream.

No wonder so many had died.

No wonder so many had disappeared without a trace.

I flicked on my Si-Tex radar system, hearing the rhythmic hum of the whirling antenna mounted above and forward. The twelve-inch screen, illuminated arm scanning, was filled with lime-green bleeps, one little explosion after another.

It looked like an armada of small boats in the chaos of retreat.

I kept a close eye on the radar screen as we plowed on through the night. Far, far in the distance, flashing white on the horizon, was the Coast Guard cutter *Dallas*, using its giant strobe lights as a beacon. Before *Sniper*, a flying fish broke the surface dripping green phosphorescence. It crashed back into the sea like a falling star. Off to starboard, broad of the bow, I saw the weak glimmer and roll of more running lights. Quickly, I went below and poured myself another mug of coffee.

It was going to be one long night.

The sea changed from the strain of darkness with dawn and in graduations of fresh light. In the east, the blackness lifted in an airy white corona, and the breeze freshened. Water changed from black to rust, then powder blue as the sun drifted over the sea, and the hulls of boats in the distance looked leached and gray in comparison to white Venus, the morning star.

"Sleep okay?"

The woman climbed up the steps to the main cabin. She wore khaki pants, pulled tight at the waist but baggy, and a burnt-orange blouse that accented the color of her eyes. For the first time, her hair was down, long and raven-black, hanging over her left shoulder. There was no puffiness in her face, and the fresh light made her look more Indian than Cuban.

"I slept quite well, thank you."

She hung over the railing of the fighting deck, looking landward.

"Is that Cuba?" As evenly as she said it, there was still just the slightest hint of excitement in her voice.

Before us, the bleak facades of pre-Castro high-rises and factories had disappeared into rolling hills and cliffs banking into the sea. On the hills was the green of bamboo and the deeper green of ficus and gumbo limbo trees.

"Yeah," I said, "that's Cuba."

I could understand her excitement. It wasn't just the mission. I knew that. It was the impact of seeing her native land after such a long absence. I knew how I had felt upon seeing the United States after my first long hitch in Nam—and America was still mine; not the victim of some raving maniac for a dictator. It was even before "our" demonstrators turned destructive.

But Cuba was no longer hers. It was a homeland of the past, like someone well loved and lost.

"Pretty country, isn't it?"

"Yes. It sure is, Androsa."

It was the first time I had called her by her first name, and instinctively, she turned toward me when I said it. Her mahogany eyes were moist, brimming, close to tears. But her guard was down only momentarily, and she turned quickly away.

"There's nothing to be ashamed of, Androsa. It's only natural that you should feel—"

She cut me off. "Mr. MacMorgan, how I feel is none of your concern." She had her back to me, trying to get her emotions under control. "And if our business relationship is to continue civilly, I would much prefer that you called me by my surname."

"Santarun, right?"

"Well, Miss Santarun might be more appropriate."

"Fine. In that case, I much prefer that you *don't* call me by my surname. Dusky will do. MacMorgan sounds too much like a hamburger chain."

The emotion was still on the surface, and she couldn't help the smile. She hurried by me, back into the cabin, calling as she went, "Do you want some more coffee?"

"Yeah. And put another pot on—that is, if you don't mind."

She came up with a fresh mug and put it on the

console in front of me. "Mr., ah, Dusky . . . I'm sorry if I am brusque. But this is a business venture. It seems to me that it's all part of your job—"

"No one likes being treated like hired help, Miss Santarun."

Her eyes flashed. "But dammit, you *are* hired help. You're being paid and paid well—far too much, to my mind."

I held my hands up. "Hold it, hold it. We were starting to get along fairly well, there. Let's just treat each other like human beings, that's all I ask. Now let's change the subject."

She took a deep breath, then sipped at her coffee. There was no mistaking the face she made. "This coffee's terrible," she said.

"You had your chance to make it. Besides, I like it terrible. It keeps me awake."

She tasted the coffee again, adjusting to the strength of it. "I guess you did have a long night. Was there any trouble?"

"Staying awake was the toughest thing, like I said. A lot of distress calls on VHF—mostly in Spanish. So I played a little game to keep my mind on what I was doing. You know how a kid counts telephone poles on a long car trip? Well, I counted boats. One way or another, we passed two hundred and fifty-seven. Busy night."

"And how far are we now from Mariel Harbor?"

"Mile and a half, two miles. It won't be long."

She strolled around the aft deck, stretching, combing through her long black hair with her fingers. "Dusky," she said, "what kind of boat is that back there, right behind us?"

I didn't even turn around. "Him? Oh, he's been tailing us ever since we got into Cuban waters. It's a gunboat. A Cuban gunboat."

The bitterness in her voice was like a living thing. "You're wrong about that, Mr. MacMorgan. It's not a Cuban gunboat. It's a *Castro* gunboat. Believe me, there's a difference. . . ."

8

The gunboat trailed us on toward the mouth of Mariel Harbor, keeping a discreet distance. In the fresh daylight, we moved over the black water past wooden swordfishing boats, their orange bouys marking miles of line—and their spritsail masts probably doubling as radio transmitters.

Abruptly, the water changed; the bottom came up from six hundred fathoms to fifteen fathoms, the hue of the sea was a soft blue jell, and you could see big fish moving among the safety of coral heads below, and the white sand, flourlike, on the bottom. From the flybridge, the water was like tinted glass and it seemed as if we were aviators at a dreamy low altitude, and the shadow of *Sniper* pressed on before us, cloudlike on the white sand.

The first view of Mariel Harbor is the picture of industry: a dozen smokestacks, a power plant, and a cement factory beneath scarred hillsides on the eastern edge of the entrance. Khaki-colored dumptrucks rumbled along dirt roads barely slowing for mule-drawn carts. And from my vantage point a half mile out to sea they looked like toys, and the exhaust from the factory stacks curved away with the wind and blended with the low mountain clouds.

"Have you ever been here before—to Mariel?"

The woman stood beside me, her eyes taking in everything as we approached. I had dropped *Sniper* down to twelve hundred RPM, lining her up with the middle channel marker, taking her in slow.

Behind us, the gunboat slowed also.

"When I was a child, yes," she said. "My father brought me here. The power plant was not built then. And the cliffs were covered with trees."

"It must have been pretty."

She nodded. "But not as pretty as other parts of Cuba."

"I've never been here, but when I was a boy I had a friend who was a very fine writer, and he told me about Mariel. He said they used to smuggle Chinese out of this harbor. One his friends lost an arm here. He didn't say how."

Her thin laughter was edged with bitterness. "So now Mariel is for smuggling Cubans. Let's hope we both keep our arms."

The entranceway to the harbor was narrow, less than a quarter mile wide, and a half-dozen American boats—cruisers, shrimp boats, and a couple of small skiffs—were anchored off the entrance in the clear water. The crews and the Cuban-Americans who had come to claim relatives were all topside in the sun, lounging and smoking nervously. It was a running tide, outgoing, and empty Coke cans and garbage bags and wine bottles flowed out to sea. A narrow paw of beach curved around on the west side of the entrance furred with tall casuarinas, which blocked our view of the harbor proper. But even above the pines I could see the masts and rigging of a thousand boats—with untold more blending into the distance.

They were all there from America.

All waiting to load with refugees and relatives.

No wonder Castro was making a half million or more a day.

I pulled downtide of one of the shrimp boats, the *Debra Jane,* and stuck both engines in idle when we were close enough to carry on a conversation.

I scanned the shrimp boat's decks for someone who looked as if he might speak English. There were six or seven people topside, all Cuban-Americans.

I turned to the woman. "Ask them why they're laying off. Ask them if we shouldn't go on into the harbor."

Androsa cupped her hands around her mouth and yelled at them in a firm Spanish alto. Immediately, everyone on deck of the *Debra Jane* was answering her one question in a barrage of rolling dialogue, everyone talking at once.

When they had finished, she said, "We're supposed to wait here for the authorities."

"Ah."

"Don't think I don't recognize that look on your

face, Mr. MacMorgan. You think it funny that 'Cubans' love to talk. And you think it's stupid that the people on that boat should take so long to give me a simple answer to a simple question."

"Something like that."

"Oh, so you admit it!" She really was surprised, and the anger left her face momentarily.

"I try to make it a point not to lie to myself. That means I only lie to myself about half the time. But as you said: you asked them a simple question. I just don't understand why Spanish people all feel obliged to talk at the same time."

"It offends you?"

"It confuses me—and I guess that's the same thing."

"It's called 'different cultures,' Mr. MacMorgan. Our society is built upon the family, and our families are built upon warmth and loyalty—and interaction. Everyone feels free to talk because we are all members of the same family." She snorted lightly, her perfect nose flaring. "Truthfully, I don't even know why I feel obligated to explain it to you. I've seen the look in your eyes from a thousand different gringos. When you grow up as an outsider in America, you come to know the look of a racist."

"So now I'm a racist?"

"Aren't you?"

"If not liking a bunch of people to talk all at the same time is being a racist, then I'm a—"

I didn't get a chance to finish, and the woman didn't get a chance to get any madder. The gunboat that had been trailing us came up close on *Sniper*'s stern, and an authoritative voice said something over a loudspeaker.

"What did he say?"

She looked smug. "Something that will appeal to the verbal economy your race seems to cherish."

"Christ, Androsa, you know how to run a thing into the ground. I understood what he said about anchoring. But I didn't get the rest of it."

The gunboat was a storm-gray cruiser, made of wood—smaller than the old PT boats. What appeared to be the captain stood beside the bow-mounted high-caliber machine gun. He wore a baggy light-blue uniform that looked like a chef's suit. His hat was light-blue, peaked and narrow, similar to the hats Japanese soldiers used to wear. He looked at me menacingly.

Androsa said, "He told you to back off and anchor immediately."

"That's all?"

"He also said we should prepare to be boarded. . . ."

We were boarded not by one captain, but two.

There was the naval officer, master of the gunboat. His name was Zapata. Captain Zapata was in his early thirties, all five feet eight inches and 145 pounds of him. He had bad teeth and a fixed expression of contempt, and he chain-smoked Partagas cigarettes. His flunkies stayed behind on the gunboat, their uniforms looking even baggier. But in their arms they cradled a weapon that I knew well: the scythe-clipped Russian AK-47 assault rifle.

And they looked as if they knew how to use them.

With Zapata was an army officer. His uniform seemed well-tailored in comparison. It was more green than khaki, and the jacket was belted with leather, shoulder and waist. He wore a sidearm and medals. I wondered if they had been one of Castro's token offerings after the revolution—or maybe he had won them in Africa.

A lot of Cuban soldiers were in Africa.

The Russians use them like German shepherds.

So they both came aboard, Zapata first, the army officer—with the unlikely name of Captain Lobo—second. Lobo was a stocky guy, something under six feet, 240 pounds maybe. Some muscle. A lot of fat. Black shadow of beard, and black eyes that betrayed the malevolence behind the cordial smile.

Some pair, Zapata and Lobo. Zapata swaggered his air of contempt up onto the aft deck of *Sniper*, and Lobo grinned his way up behind.

First impressions can fool you. I stood there loose-limbed, taking them all in, trying to smile and look harmless myself. It seemed certain that Zapata would be the one in charge.

But no, it was the grinning one.

It was Lobo. Zapata looked me up and down, his bad teeth slightly bared, and started to say something—but Lobo cut him off.

There was no doubt then who was running the show.

Lobo widened his smile, took a step closer to me, gave me the standard Spanish greeting, then asked, *"De donde es usted, Capitán?"*

He wanted to know where I was from. I looked at him blankly, shrugged my shoulders, and gestured with palm upward and turned to the woman.

"I never could understand that stuff," I said stupidly.

Her eyes showed that she wasn't fooled. "What a shame, Mr. MacMorgan. It must be dreary down there in your little crevice of existence." And without waiting for a reply—as if I had one for that—she took control of our end, talking with the two Cubans.

They wanted to see my papers. And her papers. And wouldn't we be more comfortable in the cabin with something cool to drink?

So we filed through the salon and took a seat at the little booth made of the old hatch cover, sanded silk-smooth and covered with epoxy.

My old friend Billy Mack had made it for me. But now that seemed like a long time ago.

Androsa and I sat on one side; Zapata sat scrunched between the cabin wall and the bulk of Lobo. Lobo seemed pleased to be dealing with the woman. And no wonder why. The essence of her filled the cabin. Even Zapata felt obligated to take off his little Jap hat in her presence. While Lobo talked, his black eyes leering, Zapata sat and smoked and looked at Androsa.

She didn't seem to notice.

Typically, it was a long conversation—was I her

husband (a stern "no" to that), and how was our trip over, and how many relatives did she seek. At one point, Androsa turned to me, the old aloofness in her eyes.

"Our guests would like something to drink," she said.

"I don't think the wine has properly chilled yet."

She glared at me. "This is neither the time nor the place for your perverse sense of humor, Mac-Morgan."

Angry, her E's and A's became Spanish once more.

"It's just that you're so pretty when you're mad."

She turned away as if I had said nothing. Only the slightest blush gave her away.

In the galley, I got two Hatuey beers from the ice-box, cracked them, and poured them heady into three glasses. And then I took a bottle for myself back to the booth. While Lobo gulped his beer down and Zapata sipped suspiciously at his, I took out my tin of snuff, opened it, sniffed it, and took a pinch with some ceremony. All the while, thinking:

That's right, MacMorgan. Play the jerk. Go ahead and make these guys mad so they'll send you back to home sweet Key West. Screw up this woman's chances of doing whatever it is she's supposed to do because . . . because why?

I didn't know. After all, it was her life. And if she wanted to stake herself out like a lamb on a lion hunt, it was no concern of mine. She wasn't exactly what you would call a sympathetic character; not the kind of woman I wanted to share my boat with, or my meals with—or my bed with.

Who are you trying to kid, MacMorgan? You're supposed to like the strong ones, the independent ones. And who in the hell have you met lately stronger or more self-reliant than her?

Zapata jerked me out of my little daydream.

He was making a face, acting as if the beer were laced with Tabasco.

"What's his problem?"

Androsa answered without looking away. "He says this American beer is terrible. He says it's swill that isn't fit for the pigs."

Silently, I got up and returned to the table with the empty bottle of Hatuey and placed it in front of him. His eyes widened, his face turned red. The beer he had said that wasn't fit for pigs was brewed only twenty-seven miles away in Havana. If I had slapped him across the face I couldn't have gotten a better reaction.

"MacMorgan, do you realize—"

I bumped her beneath the table with my knee. "Tell him that it's my fault. Tell him I was a fool and left it out in the sun. And tell him that everyone knows that Hatuey is one of the world's great beers."

When she got out that bit of dialogue, Zapata almost smiled, bobbing his head up and down—as if he had known all along.

"He says he'd like to try some American cigarettes—just to get the taste of bad beer out of his mouth."

The skinny little Cuban officer in the baggy blue uniform looked at me expectantly.

"I don't smoke. Do you?"

She shook her head. I still had the tin of Copenhagen in my hand. In awkward sign language, I offered him a dip of the snuff instead. He looked at Lobo, and when Lobo nodded his head, Zapata stuck a glob between his lip and bad teeth. He clicked his tongue experimentally, then eyed the ceiling, tasting the snuff.

For the new snuff dipper, there's a little matter of needing to expectorate.

A lot.

But Zapata didn't ask for a spit cup and I didn't offer. After all, they were running the show.

It was all of five minutes before the Copenhagen finally got to him. Lobo had asked Androsa for a list (in triplicate) of the relatives she wanted to take back to America. The list had to include their Cuban address and proof that they were related to Androsa.

I slid out of the booth so that she could get her papers from her bunk. And when I did, I got a good look at poor Captain Zapata. His face was red, and there was sweat on his forehead. He had sagged down into his seat, and he kept closing and opening his eyes. His Adam's apple was undulating strangely. To verify my own high regard for snuff—but more to demonstrate my innocence in the upcoming upheaval—I took out the tin of Copenhagen again and, with more ceremony, took an even larger pinch, smacking my lips.

"Next thing to mother's milk," I said loudly, offering the can to Captain Lobo. He shook his head absently. He was watching his companion closely. Zapata's head lolled back, and he closed his eyes tight as if the boat was spinning. And then, abruptly, he jumped to his feet and, knocking the considerable bulk of Lobo to one side, ran up the steps to the fighting deck as if he had important business.

"Ah . . . muy mareado. Vomito!"

And *vomito* he did.

When Androsa came back into the cabin, the sound of retching up topside was unmistakable.

"Where's Captain Zapata?" she said, glaring at me, knowing full well what had happened.

"The little guy?"

"You know damn well who I mean."

"I think he's got the vapors or something. Left without a fare-thee-well."

With a final glare, she whirled toward Captain Lobo, who was standing now, and poured out a rattling dialogue of apology.

She finished, *"El gringo capitán es sumamente estúpido!"*

Lobo didn't seem to disagree. He looked at me meanly, smiling all the while.

I smiled back.

"Well, I'm going up there to make sure he's all right!"

With a toss of her hair, the woman climbed the steps outside. It left Lobo and me alone in the cabin.

I lifted his empty glass and, in innocent sign language, asked him if he wanted another beer.

Nothing. He grinned and watched me, his wide face and mustache immobile.

"Sorry about your friend," I said, letting my tone communicate what I meant.

But my tone was wasted.

"I sincerely doubt that, Capitán MacMorgan."

It surprised me. It really did. Lobo had given me no hint that he could understand what I had been saying to Santarun. He had a heavy accent, but his words were confidently formed, well-spoken.

I held the snuff out to him. "Sure you don't want some, too?"

He chuckled, looked away. Big as he was, he was quick. He slapped the can out of my hand before I had a chance to move. The lid went twirling one way and the snuff flew across the indoor-outdoor carpeting like coffee grounds.

"Is that a no?"

For the first time, the grin disappeared from his face. He stepped closer to me, hands on hips, and growled, "You think you're quite funny, don't you, Capitán MacMorgan? Well, let me remind you that this is not the United States. I assume the woman, Miss Santarun, paid you a great deal of money to bring her here. If you want to live to spend that money, then I suggest you conduct yourself in this harbor with fitting respect. I am not your smiling neighbor, gringo. I am your superior—the moment you entered our waters, it became so." He sneered the last words. "We are no longer island slaves born to shuffle at the feet of Americanos. You are in Cuba now, Capitán MacMorgan. And don't forget it."

I still smiled. It was a necessary ploy. I wanted to see how far Castro's people could be pushed before they would allow themselves to stray into the danger zone of what might be an "international incident."

It might prove useful later to know.

And it didn't take me long to find out.

In years past, it wouldn't have happened. No official of another country would have even considered striking an American citizen—even if that citizen had acted as churlishly as I had. But now we had a President who thought an act of courage consisted of hitting a drowning rabbit with a boat paddle. Or abdicating his control over the safety of American diplomats everywhere to anyone hell-bent on holding our country hostage.

"Do you want to know when I was sure this was Cuba?" I said, still smiling.

"Not especially, *Capitán*."

"Well, I'll tell you anyway, Captain Lobo. When we pulled past that power plant over there, that's when I knew for sure. All the civilian workers were skinny. And all the soldiers guarding the beach were fat."

He slapped me so quickly, so unexpectedly, that I didn't think my next move through clearly. I felt my right hand join into a fist and swing overhand down toward Lobo's face.

I stopped it just in time, a fraction of an inch from his nose.

Lobo hadn't even flinched. "Go ahead, Capitán MacMorgan. Hit me. And after you have hit me I will have my guards escort you into Havana. Before they put you in prison you will have a very fair trial. I assure you that."

Slowly, I lowered my fist. He held all the cards. No doubt about it.

This time, anyway.

"I'm very sorry, Captain Lobo. Please accept my apology for the way I have acted." I tried to look ashamed. "I was very stupid."

The malicious grin returned to his big face. "Of course! Apology accepted! But please don't forget what I have said, Capitán MacMorgan. You might say that your life depends on remembering. . . ."

9

Mariel Harbor was a big inland lake of a port umbilicated to the sea by a natural deepwater channel. The east side of the harbor was cliffed, and industrialized with cement and power plants. But the industry gave way to higher cliffs. Bamboo and royal palms grew on the cliffs, all tapering toward the highest peak where the Cuban Naval Academy stood. It was built of native stone, four stories high, with gables and pillars, and broad stone steps that led down to the narrow road which snaked its way through the hills. North on the sheer cliff, beside the academy, were barracks of wood with tile roofs. Beyond the fortress was tropical wilderness, curving around the base of the harbor to the south end, where there were open fields and, on a distant lift of hillside, a small village.

Androsa Santarun didn't say much to me as I motored *Sniper* down the channel way to the harbor. Boats were everywhere—mostly American boats.

There were hundreds of sweeping white shrimp boats with names in broad print on their sterns: *Lucky Cracker, Georgia; Lee Wayne, Fort Myers; Pirate's Chest, Key Largo*—some of them anchored alone; others rafted in floating communities. There were schooners and skiffs and broad white yachts, all with their bows anchored into the tide—the only hint of order in the chaos of waiting vessels.

The harbor was a jumbled, polluted mess, and only the merchant seamen on the big Russian tanker tethered to the quay near the power plant seemed to move with any intensity of purpose.

"I guess I acted like a jerk back there, huh?"

She stood beside me at the cabin controls.

"There's not much doubt about that."

"Like some immature spoiled brat, wouldn't you say?"

She eyed me for a moment, studying my face. "I would say at least that."

"What did Lobo say to you when he left?"

"I really see no point in discussing what has already—"

There was a rickety houseboat ahead piloted by someone who obviously had no idea what in the hell he was doing. I swerved *Sniper* neatly to keep his blunt bow out of my beam. "I was just trying to make conversation, Miss Santarun."

She cringed slightly as the houseboat came within a foot of hitting us. For a moment, I thought she was going to yell something at the pilot. But instead she said, "Captain Lobo asked me about that scar on your face. He wanted to know why I had hired a gringo charterboat captain. He seemed suspicious of you."

"Well, I'm a little suspicious of him, too. I can't figure out why he followed us in, then boarded us first with all those other boats at the mouth of the harbor waiting."

"Maybe they had already been searched."

"That's another thing—he and Zapata hardly even took a good look at my boat. What did they do? Poke their nose into the cabin and didn't even check the engine compartments. I would hardly call it a search."

I watched her as closely as I could while running *Sniper.* I wanted to see what her reaction was. I wanted to find out if her suspicions were the same as mine: that Lobo and his cohort gave us special attention because they knew that Androsa Santarun was a spy.

But if she had any suspicions, she never let on.

"Mr. MacMorgan," she said, "please don't ask me any questions, because I have no answers. Just promise me this—that you will never again jeopardize my . . . my attempts to get my father out of Cuba with your silly jokes."

"I thought you hated the Castro Cubans. It seems to me that what I did—"

"I do hate them!" She said it fiercely. She meant it. "I hate every single thing they stand for. Look at that!" She swept her hand toward the tropical wilderness beyond the Naval Academy. "Never was there a place so beautiful as Cuba. But Castro did not take it from Batista to give it to the Cuban people. He took it for *himself*. I do hate them, and that is exactly why I don't want to take the chance of playing silly jokes. It could . . . could ruin everything.''

We had been told to anchor on the west side of the harbor, so I pointed *Sniper* toward one of the few chunks of open water, away from the flood of other boats. A broad peninsula of white sand and Australian pines separated the port from a finger of bay, and on the peninsula was a ragged military outpost. There was a colony of barrack houses built of concrete block and painted a shabby blue or bleached pink. Some of the roofs were tiled, others were thatched. Just to the south of the huts was a small but modern aircraft control tower and an amphibious landing strip. Absently, I wondered how much it had cost the Russians. Beyond the glass quadrangular of control tower was a steel pier where two antiquated gunboats were moored, and above that, in a clearing, was a baseball diamond with a chicken-wire backstop. Guards patrolled the beach with emaciated German shepherds, and there were bunkers beyond the beach, poorly camouflaged.

I nosed *Sniper* uptide, and before I went forward to drop the hook, I turned to the woman.

"You're right," I said. "Giving that Zapata character snuff was a rotten joke. And I promise I'll never do it again. But you have to admit—it *was* kind of funny. Did you see him start to sweat and hold onto the table like the boat was spinning? I thought he was going to break a leg trying to get out of that cabin. . . ."

Androsa turned abruptly away from me and walked back toward the starboard fighting chair.

I watched her trying hard to repress a smile as she went.

And so the waiting began.

We were just one of fifteen hundred American boats in Mariel Harbor waiting on some word of the relatives we wanted to take back to America.

Androsa Santarun knew all the steps in the procedure after her talk with Captain Lobo. First, her triplicate papers with her father's name would go to the Cuban immigration authorities. They would process the papers and decide if he was eligible to go to America—"eligible" meaning that he was not of military age, that he was not a physician or government employee, and that he was not an "enemy of the people."

The last requirement was pretty vague, of course. And could be used to stop anybody from leaving that they damn well didn't want to leave.

After the papers were processed and okayed, the relatives supposedly would be sent to the waiting boats.

But the woman said she knew otherwise. She said it was a lot more complicated than that. She told me about it at dinner that night, in the longest conversation we had had the whole trip. That's one thing about a boat. People crammed together in close quarters long enough either turn murderous, or they find a common plateau of conversation and acceptance that will at least make the trip bearable.

Happily enough, she had chosen the latter alternative.

I had spent the hot afternoon leaning into the narrow confines of the engine room, puttering with this, changing that, adding seals and new belts where they were needed. Every now and then I'd break for a cold beer, wipe my face with a towel, and sit in the shade to watch the Cuban patrol and taxi boats idle between anchorages. The woman had changed from pants and blouse to a striking white bikini that had men on the boats nearest ours running for their binoculars. As aloof as Androsa Santarun was, she seemed totally unconcerned with the impact of her physical appearance.

And the impact was considerable.

She was a woman of length and curves: long black hair streaming toward the ripe flexure of high, round buttocks and the grace of long legs. The white suit emphasized the darkness of her, and her ribs undulated promisingly toward the wide, firm impetus of breasts, barely covered by the skimpy top.

It was all I could do not to stare at her when she walked past me to rummage in the cabin for a book, or a cold drink, or a towel.

But I made myself; forced myself to act oblivious to her sexuality, knowing that if she did feel my eyes upon her—and she would—that I would be dismissed as just one more horny son of a bitch.

And that's when I knew that she had me.

Any time you start measuring your reactions to please or impress someone, then you know their effect on you is something other than commonplace.

Great, MacMorgan. Just great. You've been with this woman how long? Little more than twenty-four hours. You see her kill a man coldly and professionally, and you have sat like a kid in a corner while she treated you like hired help. So why the special interest? There is a woman in Chicago, another in New York, and the best of them all back in Key West—every one of them beautiful, intelligent, eager, and one hell of a lot easier to get along with. So why get taken in by this one?

I really didn't know *why* I was playing little games for her approval.

Maybe it was the way she had acted when she saw the man with his throat cut on *Storm Nest.*

Maybe it was that hint of vulnerability beneath the black ice of her eyes in that singular moment. Or the way she had leaned against me for support. Or the small-ness of her beneath my hands, or . . . hell, I just didn't know.

So I worked hard all afternoon in the sun. And tried to ignore the vision in the white suit. And tried harder to force the urge to seek her favor from my head.

Across the harbor, half a mile of water and several hundred boats away, I could hear the voice of Cuban authority over a big PA system somewhere north of the Naval Academy. On the beach of the peninsula, only a hundred yards away, the guards still patrolled the area with their AK-47s and their shepherds, watching for Cubans who might try to make a swim for one of the American boats.

The place didn't exactly exude friendliness.

For supper that night, I had thawed out four sizable lobster tails. I had caught plenty the season before, and now was a good time to enjoy them. Mariel Harbor, it was easy to see, didn't offer much else in the way of luxury.

At sundown, I went for a short swim, toweled off, and then went below to set water to boiling for the lobster. In another pot, I dumped in a stick of real butter and set the alcohol burner on dead low.

Lobster and what else? I thought for a moment. If I was alone, what else would I fix?

Garlic bread, toasted. Maybe a salad. That's all. And if the woman didn't like it, she could fix her own supper.

I cleaned off the galley table and added plates. Then I went to work on the salad, cutting plenty of sweet onion into it.

"How was the water?"

She came down the cabin stairs, all long legs and swell of womanhood beneath the suit. Her high Indian cheeks were bronzed by the sun, and her hair was shiny with tanning oil.

"Water's dirty—too damn dirty for swimming."

She grabbed a chunk of onion as she swept past me and chewed it while she spoke. "I thought about going in, but . . . well, I was afraid there might be sharks around."

"Sharks?" I looked down into her mahogany eyes. For the first time, she looked relaxed. Even sleepy. "I imagine most of the sharks in this harbor left when they heard you were here. No, the most dangerous thing about that water is staph infection. When I got out, I washed my ears with some of that cheap rum under the sink."

"So that's what I smelled."

"And you just thought I was drunk again, right?"

She fished out another piece of onion from the salad. "Isn't that the way you charterboat captains live? You make enough money to get good and drunk, and then you don't go back to work until the booze runs out. That's what everyone says, anyway."

I dropped the four lobster tails into the sputtering water, added a little salt, then covered them. "Right. It's all true. Nothing I like better than getting hopelessly drunk. How about you?"

"Do you have to work at being so sarcastic, Mr. MacMorgan? Or does it just come naturally?"

"It depends on who I'm talking to. And you're supposed to call me Dusky. Remember?"

When the lobster was done, I butterflied them and set slivers of fresh lime on the table. The woman surprised me by asking for beer every time I got up to get one. It wasn't a meal for forks and knives and the dainty attack those things imply. It was a meal to eat with your hands, with hot butter and garlic bread; it was a meal that required plenty of napkins.

When we had finished, Santarun surprised me by gathering the dishes and pots together in the sink

and putting water on to boil—for coffee and dishwater.

She saw the way I raised my eyes at that.

"Are you surprised that I'm volunteering to
work?" she said, knowing full well that I was.

"Shocked might be a better word."

"Actually, I want to do the dishes as a show of
good faith; good faith because I'm about to tell you
something that really might shock you."

"Hold off telling me until the end of the trip. That
way you can do all the dishes as a sign of good
faith." ·

"I'm afraid I have no desire to show that much good
faith." She laughed lightly. I studied to see if the sudden friendliness was forced, and decided—probably
because of the four beers she had had—that it wasn't.
"Actually, Dusky, it has to do with my conversation
earlier with that Cuban soldier—Captain Lobo."

And that's when she told me about the preliminary
steps it took to get a relative out of Cuba.

"But once the papers have been processed, and my
father has been approved, I'm sure they're not going
to just bring him down to this boat and wave goodbye," she continued.

"What makes you think that?"

She hesitated for a moment while she squirted
soap into the dishwater and went to work on the
plates. "For one thing, I've been listening to other
Cuban-Americans talking on your radio. Some of
them have been over here before, and they've talked
with the refugees in Key West. Once the relatives

have been approved, the first thing the Castro regime does is confiscate their homes and their property. And then they send them to refugee camps—"

"Which, I imagine, are more like concentration camps."

"Exactly."

"Well, that's not completely unexpected. I mean, Castro isn't exactly known as a humanitarian." I nodded toward the stack of dishes. "So why the unexpected goodwill gesture?"

"Wait," she said. "There's more. You don't have to listen to that radio for long to realize that we're in for a long stay here. That's the point I was trying to make. Castro's people are holding the refugees in those concentration camps for a reason. This afternoon, while you were working on the engine, I watched them loading the refugees through your binoculars. The dock's across the harbor—Captain Lobo called it Pier Three. Do you have any idea how many boats they loaded in eight hours?"

I shook my head. "You can herd a lot of people onto a deck in eight hours."

"You could—but they didn't. Only two boats were loaded. That's what I'm trying to get at. Castro *wants* it to be slow. *I* think he wants us all to stay here until we've eaten all our food and spent all our money."

Suddenly it dawned on me. "So now I see why you're being so nice all of a sudden—"

"If that's an insult, I'm afraid—"

I smiled at her. "Face it, Santarun. You haven't exactly been Miss Congeniality on this trip. But now you're afraid I'm going to get tired of waiting around here in Mariel Harbor after a week or so, pull anchor, and head back to Key West. So now you're trying to charm me into some verbal agreement—"

"I am not! I'm just trying to tell you the facts!"

She glared at me. It was getting so I liked that glare. She had pulled on a baggy blue shirt over her swim suit, and she had her hands on her hips, leaning toward me like an angry kid.

"And you're trying to cover the facts with all the sugar and spice you can."

"MacMorgan, you are so pigheaded! I was just trying to explain to you that we might have to stay here in Mariel a little longer than we had planned, but you have to read all sorts of devious motives into it."

"But you *do* want me to agree to stay until your business is finished—right?"

"Yes!"

"Even if it takes a month or more?"

"Of course!"

"And even if we run out of food?"

"You were paid to bring me here, then take me back when I was done . . . when I had my father!"

She had slipped and she knew it. Quickly, she busied herself with cleaning up the galley. She had played the role of the daughter seeking her father so well that, for a time, I had wondered if she really did have a father still in Cuba. Now was the time to blow her cover—and mine—if I wanted. Why not get things out in the open? After all, couldn't we work better as a team?

I thought about it. I really did. And I came damn close to putting all my cards on the table.

The only thing that stopped me was my promise to Norm.

He had ordered me to stay neutral. I was supposed to watch and report back. If things got too rough for the woman I could step in—but then and only then.

I got up from the booth, stretched, then reached over and put my hand on her shoulder. I expected her to flinch, but she didn't.

"I'm sorry, Androsa."

She kept her head down, running a dishcloth around the little alcohol stove. "It's okay. You're right. I have been pretty nasty to you."

"That's true."

She gave me a warning glance that said, "Do you want to argue some more?"

I didn't, so I hurried on, "All the lockers are filled with canned goods. We have ten pounds of rice, plenty of fish, and ten cases of beer. When the food is all gone—and we probably have enough for five or six weeks—then we go. Agreed?"

She reached as if to give my hand a sisterly pat, but stopped halfway.

"Agreed," she said.

Outside, the sky was blurred with smog from the factories, and the military had big runway searchlights scanning the harbor. Boats in the distance stood out in blue silhouette in the vacillating darkness, and, standing on the aft deck, I could hear snatches of rapid Spanish drifting across the water.

Somewhere, calypso music played from a radio. It seemed out of place in the somberness of Mariel Harbor.

I reached into my shirt pocket, took an after-dinner dip, then collected a blanket, pillow, and flashlight and climbed up to the flybridge and lay down.

I had only gotten about three hours of sleep after the long run from Key West. And I was tired. Damn tired.

But across the harbor, I knew, were thousands of people even more tired than I. They were the refugees, homeless in their camps, all hopes fixed on the dream of America.

Lying there beneath the veiled stars I thought of them, and I wondered what America, already choking with heavy welfare rolls and unemployment, was going to do with a hundred thousand non-English-speaking expatriates—many of them a cross-section of criminals, spies, and Castro castoffs. And I wondered what effect the worst of them would have on the destinies of the innocent.

Even with the smog, it was a nice night: a cool land breeze blew down out of the high country. I began to think of the woman, and fell into a restless sleep.

10

There was the scream of siren.

And shots.

A machine gun, and it wasn't far away.

It slipped into my dreams like some malevolent creature, and pulled me down into those memories that, even in reality, were nightmares.

They're dead, Dusky. All dead. Three bodies scattered like broken toys. . . .

And then the shots came from the perimeter of a base camp up a jungle river long ago and far away, and I was leading a watch of SEALs neck-deep in black water into a firefight that could only end one way—with Charlie hunting us with sampans and converted assault skiffs, and us knowing even before we fired our first round that it was going to be one hell of a deadly swim back to the World, and some of us weren't going to make it. . . .

And then I suddenly was awake.

The searchlight from the military outpost on the peninsula was tunneling through the darkness, pounding out an area of stark daylight on a patch of water a hundred yards or so from *Sniper.* The water was a phlegm green where the searchlight scanned, and I could see the white flare of spray which marked the trajectory of bullets coming from the beach.

I jumped to my feet, throwing off the blanket, then swung down the ladder onto the deck.

The woman was already up, leaning out anxiously over the railing trying to see what the Cubans were shooting at.

"Get down, dammit!"

I jerked her roughly down onto the deck. The light swept across *Sniper,* showing her face pale, wide-eyed. She wore a white T-shirt and sheer panties which, in the brief shock of light, showed her as she would look naked.

"Those bastards are crazy," I said. "They're not even sure what they're shooting at, and one dead Cuban-American woman isn't going to bother them one way or the other. So stay down, got it?"

She nodded quickly. She was shaking, and it wasn't from the cool night wind. I knew what was on her mind. She thought that this was it: Castro's way of getting rid of one American spy.

When the searchlight had crossed back over *Sniper,* I poked my head under the railing and followed the path of the beam.

And then I saw it.

A human figure swimming for his life. In the brilliance of the beam, steam came up off the water, and the swimmer appeared oil-black. He was doing a ragged, overhand crawlstroke. He swam with his head up, legs way too low, and I knew that only fear and adrenaline could provide the strength it would take for him to make it the sixty yards to the nearest boat—my boat, *Sniper.*

"Why don't they just send a boat out and arrest him?" the woman wondered out loud, angry, almost yelling it.

"Oh, they're sending a skiff out right now—see the light over by the wharf? But they don't want to arrest him. They want to make an example out of him. They want to kill him."

The searchlight was full on the refugee. It was pathetic. He tried to disappear underwater once, but he was no swimmer, and he came back up only a few seconds later.

Poppa-poppa-pop . . .

It was a sound I knew well.

The assault rifles swept across him in an explosion of spray. One of the slugs jerked him back and swung him around. It must have hit him in the shoulder, because he floundered in the water with one weak arm pawing for survival.

In that harsh steaming light, he looked like a dog abandoned at sea, finally ready to give up.

I felt the anger move through me like a fever. Those bastards. It was something the soldiers would laugh about in the morning. Who was the best shot?

Which of them could cut a notch in their Russian rifles?

Even as I watched, my hands began to move as if they had minds of their own, stripping off my T-shirt, working at my belt.

"Dusky, what are you doing!"

"I think I might go for a little swim."

She pulled herself close beside me, drawing my head around to face her.

"Dusky, there's nothing you can do. Can't you see that? My God, don't try something so stupid! You can't save him—"

"That's right, I can't. But dammit, I can try."

She was right, of course. He was a goner. One way or another, they would get him.

But at least I could try to spoil their fun.

Wearing only underwear I dove headlong into the harbor—head down, hands joined into fists to punch a good hole in the water. A nice quiet dive. I swam strong and smooth, eyes up, watching, in a lifesaver's crawl.

The poor bastard was still using the one evasive tactic he had. He'd come up for a quick breath, wave his one good arm as if to surrender, then push himself back under when the soldiers started shooting again.

They weren't about to let him surrender.

Poppa-poppa-pop . . .

More gunfire. Absently, I wondered how long it would take a company of good Marines to bust these

Cuban amateurs into submission and work their way to downtown Havana.

About as long as it would take me to swim to the wounded refugee, probably.

As I drew closer, I could hear him splashing and gasping, moaning in pain.

"Yo rendir! Por favor, yo rendir!"

But the Cuban soldiers weren't about to have their sleep interrupted for nothing. They weren't about to let him surrender.

They fired again, the slugs throwing green wakes into the water.

I was right on the perimeter of the big beam of searchlight. I exhaled completely, took five good deep breaths, then dove. I had my target marked well.

But even if I didn't, I would have found him anyway. It was a night of neap moon, and the water was filled with the billions of little microorganisms that glow like fireflies at the slightest stir. And the green sparkle of phosphorescence marked my objective as I swam in long gliding strokes beneath the surface.

It's weird underwater at night.

And even stranger when the trajectories of bullets throw glowing half moons ahead of you.

In the eerie radiance of bioluminescence, I could see his legs struggling in an awkward scull kick. His one arm hung limply at his left side. He lifted slightly, then threw his right arm upward, pushing himself underwater.

I had to figure that he had taken a pretty good breath. For his sake, I hoped he had.

And when he came down, eyes squinched shut, teeth bared with strain, I took him by the shoulders, turned him around, and grabbed him firmly across the chest.

It scared him. Shocked the hell out of him. And I knew he thought that a shark had him.

I put my mouth right against his ear and yelled, *"Amigo!"* The water distorted the word, but it still came out as that of a human voice. He struggled briefly, then resigned himself to holding his breath.

And hoping.

It's not easy pulling someone else along underwater. You have to fight the buoyancy of two bodies and, all the while, try to build up enough gliding momentum to make some distance.

I knew that I had to cover at least twenty yards, or we were both dead.

But there was no way that he had the wind for it. I felt his chest heave, demanding that his brain let him breathe. And then he began to struggle again— this time, a life-and-death struggle.

I exhaled slightly, trying to rid my lungs of any carbon dioxide build-up, and then I forced my mouth down over his while pinching his nose shut. I exhaled sharply, trying to fill his lungs with some good air. And when I did, my fingers touched a sickly mat of damaged flesh on the left side of his head.

So his shoulder wasn't the only thing that had slowed a slug.

He stopped struggling momentarily. And I knew the charge of air had done him some good.

Pull . . . frog-kick . . . glide, then pull again before the momentum is halted.

When I knew that we had escaped the glare of searchlight, I surfaced. The refugee's head hung limply on his shoulder, but he was still alive.

In my bad Spanish, I whispered hoarsely in his ear, *"Respirar! Respirar!"*

His chest heaved and he took a couple of shallow breaths. And when he was ready, I pulled him down again, swimming hard for the black silhouette of *Sniper.*

I could hear the *whir* of a small boat propeller, and a shaft of light with milky radiance swept through the green water, then moved away.

I had to surface once more before the final swim to the temporary safety of my boat.

They would get him. Sooner or later. Unless . . .

I couldn't waste energy thinking about the possibilities. The Cuban skiff was circling in the area where I had first jerked the refugee under.

That was good. Maybe they thought he was dead. Shot or drowned.

There were soldiers in the skiff, faces lighted by the white glow of stern light. They waved their rifles around menacingly, and I could hear their loud laughter. It was great sport to them. Hunt down the unarmed man. Shoot and shoot until a lucky shot finally hit him, then search for the trophy—a body, floating.

If I ever get the chance, you bastards will be the first to go. . . .

When we were safely away, I pulled the refugee around to the starboard side of *Sniper*, using my boat as a shield from the searchlight on the military outpost.

In the thin night light, I could see that the left side of his head was a mass of blood. It was amazing that he had lasted as long in the water as he did.

"Dusky? Dusky, is that you?"

It was Androsa. She leaned over the railing, peering down into the darkness.

"There's a boarding ladder in the stern locker, under the life jackets. Get it."

She hurried away while I tried to catch my breath. It had been one hell of a swim.

When the ladder was down and secured, I got the refugee across my shoulder, then pulled myself up onto the deck, trying to stay low. The woman was smart. She hadn't turned on a single light. But then I realized that probably wasn't the smart thing after all. The vessels nearest *Sniper*—the closest about two hundred yards away—all had their lights on, awakened by the shooting.

Quickly, I carried him down into the cabin. He was moaning now, spitting up water hot on my back. I put him down on the forward berth and swung his feet up.

"Hit the main switch," I said.

The woman had followed me in. She stood close

behind me, her hand on my arm, looking around my shoulder.

"What? But they'll see—"

"Damn it, Androsa, turn on some lights. It's the only way we're *not* going to look suspicious."

When the overhead lamp came on, I got my first good look at the man I had saved. He was something over six feet tall, bony but not skinny. He wore cheap sackcloth pants and a shirt of the same material. His skin was light, his face that of the pure-blooded Basque, and he had a narrow mustache and a seven- or eight-day growth of black beard.

I reached beneath the berth and took out a square of green tarp. When I had it spread out, I rolled him over on it, then pulled off the bedsheets before the blood had a chance to soak through. He wasn't bleeding profusely; not now anyway. But his hair was so matted that I couldn't get a good look at the head wound.

"Here. I brought this."

The woman shoved the first-aid kit in front of me. And then: "No, don't wipe it like that. You should pat the blood off . . . here, let me."

I stood up, giving her room to work. When I did, she did a double take. At first, I thought it was because I wore only the sodden underwear. But then I knew what she was looking at, her dark eyes locked on my hips.

"My God, what . . . how did you get that?"

"A big dusky shark took me for a surface lure one night."

I nodded toward the man who lay on the tarp. "But he's the one who needs help now. My shark story can wait. This scar isn't going anyplace."

She worked on him calmly and professionally, cleaning and bandaging the wounds.

"He's very badly hurt," she said.

"Well, maybe the Cubans will let a doctor look at him before they send him off to prison—"

"No!"

She said it with such intensity, such determination, that it took me aback.

"Androsa, even if the soldiers decide that he drowned and call off the search, the authorities will still find him when they make the final search before we leave."

Her eyes were resolute. "Dusky, we can't let Castro's people get him again. Not after what he's been through—and not after what you went through to save him. Besides, if they find out that we helped him, I'll never get my father. Never!"

It was a sound enough argument, but she was holding something back. I could see it just beyond the glimmer of her mahogany eyes—there was something she wasn't telling me.

And that's when I began to suspect.

But I didn't push it.

"Okay," I said. "Fine. We'll hide him as best we can."

She sighed, relieved.

I took another long look at the refugee, then climbed the cabin steps topside. Out on the harbor, the search was still underway. A gunboat had joined the skiff, idling back and forth, working its way away from *Sniper.*

There was no laughter now.

Their trophy was nowhere to be found.

I grabbed a towel, stripped off my underwear, and dried off. The green glow of my Rolex watch said it was nearly three a.m.

Some rude awakening.

I hung my shorts over the stainless-steel wheel to dry, then pulled on the good dryness of khaki pants and T-shirt. It wouldn't do to be soaking wet when the soldiers started their search of boats.

And I knew they would. Sooner or later, if the body didn't appear, they would have to.

It surprised me when I heard the sound of a weak male voice coming from the cabin. I had told Androsa to call me if the refugee regained consciousness. And just as I was about to go below to see if he had anything to say, I stopped myself.

Maybe she hadn't called me for a reason.

Barefooted, I made my way along the starboard walkway forward. The port above the master berth was screened from bugs, but open for the breeze. I stretched out over and in, looking down into the cabin.

I could see them both clearly. The white T-shirt did a bad job of hiding Androsa's nakedness, and she had the man's head cradled in her lap. She spoke in whispered Spanish: rapid, inquisitive.

He was so weak that he could do nothing else but whisper. His words came in agonizing gasps. And I knew he didn't have much longer to live. Every now and then he would clutch at the bandage on his head in a spasm of pain. When he did speak, it seemed to be a rambling montage of nouns, all in delirious disorder.

Androsa did her best to calm him, stroking his head with a damp cloth and questioning him softly. There was a gentleness to her that I had only suspected.

He spasmed again, and she held him tightly.

"Halcón . . . Halcón . . . no, no, ustedes hermanastro . . ."

He said this last in a hoarse shout, rolling out of Androsa's arms in his pain, and then, mercifully, was quiet. Sobbing quietly, the woman pulled his eyelids shut and covered his face with the tarp.

Quickly, I made my way back to the aft deck, his feverish last words echoing in my brain.

Hermanastro? What in the hell did *hermanastro* mean? *Herman* was "brother," but what was . . .

Androsa came onto the deck stoically, her eyes already dry.

"He's gone," she said simply.

"I'm sorry."

She touched my face with her hand. "You did more than most men would have done—Cuban or otherwise."

It was an honest bitterness I felt; honest because it seems that, no matter how hard you try, no matter how desperately you fight, death is always the unchallenged victor. "Right," I said. "Absolutely. I'm a real goddam ace. . . ."

11

It didn't take me long to verify that the dead "refugee" was really one of the Cuban-American CIA agents sent to Mariel Harbor to rescue General Halcón.

While Androsa stayed up on the deck, trying to recover while keeping an eye on the progress of the search boats, I went back below.

"I'll take care of the body," I told her.

"But how? What will you do?"

She looked tired, depressed. There was a strange emptiness in her eyes. She still wore the baggy T-shirt and brief panties. I put my arm around her, and she sagged against my chest. Her hair smelled lightly of tanning oil, and her skin was soft.

"You need some sleep. You look tired."

"Oh, I feel so damn . . . helpless!"

I thought she was going to cry again, but she didn't.

"You're anything but helpless. Just tired, that's all." I patted her head gently. "I'll take care of things down in the cabin. When I'm done, I'll call you. And then you can get back to sleep."

She looked up into my face. Her lips were moist and parted, and there was a soft sleepiness to her face. She looked very kissable, and I felt something in my stomach stir, but now was not the time.

She said, "Dusky, when we started this trip I . . . I hated you. And I hated the idea of having to be on this boat with you. But now I'm glad. You aren't like I thought, and . . . and I'm glad. . . ."

She left the sentence unfinished, sighing.

"I've wondered about that—why did you hate me? I've always thought I was a pretty swell guy."

She almost smiled. "Do you want me to be honest?"

"Sure."

"Well, so many Anglos come to Mariel to get rich. They charge my people unbelievably high prices to bring them here. My people had to mortgage their homes, sell their jewelry, and . . . well, I just don't like people who try to make money on the desperation of others."

"I didn't come cheap," I said. It wasn't true—but I had to say it.

"I know, I know." She stopped and looked at me. "But no matter how hard I try now, I can't make myself believe that you came for the money. No one else would have jumped in to save . . . save that poor man." She was studying me now, the way someone might study an enigmatic painting. "Dusky, somehow, you give me the feeling that you *care*. I never expected that—never, not from some big blond-haired charter-boat captain. But I'm . . . I'm glad. . . ."

Her face was tilted toward mine. It was a face from Gauguin; a dream face draped in a black sheen of hair. I felt myself drifting toward her, wanting her lips, wanting to hold her, wanting to take her as a part of me—to strip away that final reserve which was the mystery of her and discover the woman inside.

Abruptly, she turned her face aside.

"I'd better keep an eye on those . . . those search boats," she said. Her breathing seemed strangely labored, and as she turned sideways I could see the points of her nipples erect beneath the thin T-shirt.

"Right," I said. "Yeah, you better do that."

"And you'll take care of—"

"Right."

I went below and quickly lashed the tarp and bloody sheet around the body. His face was waxy, peaceful in death. And, as always, I felt that odd sense of loss in the face of death, like a member of some huge fleet who looks out and sees that boats are being quietly abandoned. That seemed to describe death better than anything else. Personalities don't die, they just disappear; abandon their vessels for—for what?

Who the hell knows. Or cares.

I pushed back the screen of the overhead port and shoved the body up onto the foredeck.

One of the gunboats had pulled up beside a big shrimp boat three hundred yards downtide. They figured, probably, if he had drowned his body would have drifted in that direction. The soldiers had the boat's searchlight fixed on the faces of the Cuban-Americans aboard the shrimp boat, and they were asking them questions in loud Spanish.

I got all the spare chain I had from the forward locker—about fifty pounds' worth—and took a roll of wire, the side-cuts, and my spare thirty-pound anchor.

Except for my rock anchor, it was all the extra ground tackle I had, and if another squall came blasting across the Straits like the last one . . . well, it would be time to head for deep water and break out the canvas sea anchor.

But I couldn't worry about that now.

Before I climbed out onto the deck, I fished my black watch sweater and wool cap out of my sea bag and pulled them on.

It was no time to be seen.

I tossed the chain over one shoulder, then pulled myself up through the porthole.

Wiring weights to a corpse is not what you call pleasant duty. I hitched the first link firmly to his right ankle, then wrapped the chain around him barber-pole-like, then added more wire at the neck. The wire snugged up with grisly ease. When the chain was in place, I secured the anchor to his stomach.

Staying low, I pulled him across the foredeck. I didn't want to risk making a loud splash. I positioned his head so that it hung off the deck. Bracing my legs as best I could, I got down on my stomach and began to lower him over.

What would the total weight be?

One hundred and seventy pounds plus eighty?

In that area.

One hell of a heavy load.

The stripping around the deck cut into my arms and my shoulders creaked with the strain. Hand over hand, I lowered him head first into the black water.

He went down in a swirl of green phosphorescence, sparkling into the depths, as if he fell through stars.

I looked up. The gunboat was finished with the shrimp boat. It used no running lights. And it was coming our way.

So let them come. What they were looking for was now five fathoms down, already disappearing into the soft mud bottom.

I slid back through the porthole, pulling the screen shut behind me.

The woman was still back on the fighting deck. So I had time to check what I wanted to check.

I pulled off the sweater and cap and stuffed them back into my sea bag. The biographies Norm Fizer had given me were well hidden. I pulled back the indoor-outdoor carpet above the forward bilge. The bilge was dry and empty—except for one spare marine battery. It was the best kind of hiding place—no one wants to mess with fifteen pounds of wet-cell.

But this was no ordinary battery.

Using my Gerber knife, I pried the whole top off it, hearing water slosh in the fake cap compartments. The file was in there; the biography file and more. There was my Randall attack-survival knife, the knife that had saved my life—and taken others—more than once. And beneath that were the seven one-pound blocks of RDX plastic explosives: Cyclonite, the deadliest military-strength explosive available. And that wasn't my only offensive option. I stuck my arm into the bilge and felt the roof of the compartment.

The handmade aluminum arrows were all there, taped in place. They were precision instruments that fitted the Cobra crossbow I had disassembled and stored innocuously in the engine compartment.

The file was rolled into a tight tube. I slid the rubber bands off and leafed through the pages until I had found what I was looking for. Even without the head wound, it was easy to see that the man who was chained thirty feet beneath *Sniper* was the same man in the black-and-white glossy photo:

Ovillo Gomez, 37. Divorced, 2 dep. (girls 13, 10) living with subject's former spouse Aurora (Abeta) Gomez (which see). Nat. Cit. Aug. 1966, Grad. Yale June '71. PBK, Dean's List, 2Lt. ROTC. Recruited by Organization Sept. '71, 6 Promotions (which see). . . .

It was all straight from the sterile computers at the sterile headquarters in Washington, where a man's life, like certain chemicals, can be readily distilled into a few nouns, and where even honors are worthy only of abbreviation.

I wondered if they had a printout on me, and knew, of course, that they did. Empty facts and figures, the biographical skeleton of me. I was surprised to find myself suddenly furious; mad at the facts-and-figures bastards in Washington; bitter at the truth that I too had become nothing more than a killing pawn for the "Organization," one more name on a list.

In childish protest, I ripped up the photo and short biography of the late Ovillo Gomez. I wouldn't give the computer goons a chance to stamp *Killed in Line of Duty* across them.

And I hoped that, someday, someone would do the same for me. . . .

Captain Lobo was in a surly mood when his gunboat finally rumbled up beside *Sniper*.

His fat face glistened with sweat as if hunting down a corpse were the hardest work of all. The snap on his holster was undone, the little Russian revolver ready.

I had gone back out to the aft deck to stand with Androsa and await their arrival. One by one, they were searching boats. And I knew that our time would come.

Almost on queue, the gunboat's searchlight painted us in its stark glare. Androsa shielded her eyes, then looked away.

"Hey," I said. "Are you going to be able to handle this?"

"You just take care of yourself, Captain."

"You're trembling."

"Only because I'm cold."

"It might be that outfit you're wearing—not that I don't like it."

She looked absently at the long T-shirt she wore as a nightgown. "Oh," she said. "I'd forgotten." She tried briefly to cover herself with her hands, then realized how ridiculous it was. "The boat's coming—I don't have time to—"

"I've got an old robe I'll lend you."

By the time I got back up and helped her put on the robe, Lobo's crew was making lines fast to *Sniper*'s cleats. It was the same twosome: Lobo, looking surly; Zapata only grim, like some diseased hawk. But even in Lobo's mood, the expression of amusement was pasted onto his face. Only now the grin was more of a sneer.

"You are up very late, señorita," Lobo said, coming aboard, trying to straighten his uniform and hat all at the same time. And then to me: "Ah, and you too, *Capitán*? May I ask why?"

"Gunshots seem to give me insomnia, Captain Lobo."

"Ah?" And then the broad smile: "So we are all up when some of us would much rather be in bed. No?"

He looked meaningfully at the woman. If he wanted a game, I was happy to play along. I reached out and put my hand on Androsa's shoulder. "I just wish that was true," I said.

As I hoped she would, she jerked away from my grasp.

Lobo laughed with ugly delight. "So! A hot-blooded one, this? Hah!"

Zapata had said nothing. The spotlight was still aimed at *Sniper*, and he stood in the brief shadow of the cabin. Increasingly, I was becoming aware that the crew of the gunboat was giving me special attention, eyeing every move I made. Their automatic weapons were in evidence, but it was more than just a military attention. Their faces seemed amused, expectant. Some of them even smiled, looking from me to Zapata.

And then I put two and two together.

Nowhere does rumor travel as fast as among a platoon of soldiers. They had probably heard all about my run-in with Zapata, and, from the looks on their faces, they thought it a pretty funny story. I was the Americano who had embarrassed their captain. And I imagined Zapata to be something less than a popular officer—even before the incident.

Now he had become a joke.

I looked at Zapata standing in the shadows, smiled—and got a glare for my trouble.

It was something to keep in mind.

I turned to Lobo. "You never did say, Captain, what your people were shooting at."

The grin edged with sneer again. "That's right,

Capitán. I did not. But we have no secrets—despite what your newspapers say about us, huh?" He didn't wait for an answer. He continued, "A very foolish man, an escaped criminal, tried to swim to an American boat tonight. It was foolish because, as you have seen, our beaches are well guarded and he had no chance of success. Unfortunately, one of our navy's officers ordered the guards to—how do you say it?—'open guns' before they had a chance to see *which* boat he was trying to swim to. So now we are all awake because of an officer *muy estúpido.*"

I didn't have to turn around and look at Zapata to know which officer Lobo was talking about. Poor Captain Zapata had had one very bad day.

"The man got away?"

Lobo made a noncommittal gesture with his hands. "The guards say the man went underwater and did not come back up—but who is to say? It is very dark, no? And we have found no body. So now we search."

"You're welcome to look around my boat if you like."

For a microsecond, the mask of congeniality disappeared from Lobo's face—and I saw just what a ruthless son of a bitch he really was. He said, "Thank you, *Capitán,* but we do not need your permission to search this boat."

He signaled the soldiers waiting on the gunboat, and three of them came aboard, their AK-47s ready. While two of them looked over the engine compartment with flashlights, Captain Lobo went below with the third. They would make a thorough search—but for a man. Nothing else.

Or so I hoped.

I moved over closer to the woman. She had her head down, as if tired. But then I realized that she had her head down for a reason—she was looking at something. Zapata still glared at me. Slowly, nonchalantly, she turned away from him. I put my arm around her, holding tight, telling her with the firmness of my grip that I did not want her to pull away. It was a reassurance and a question in one; a question she answered by letting the robe open briefly, then pulling it tightly around her.

And then I knew what she had been looking at.

On her T-shirt, low and off to the left where she had cradled the head of Ovillo Gomez, was a black blotch of blood.

I patted her shoulder and said nothing, thinking all the while: *You'd better come up with something good, MacMorgan—just in case. If they see that bloodstain, both of you are going to spend the next forty years playing one-on-one with ratshit in some Cuban prison. . . .*

Lobo came out of the cabin preceded by the soldier. In his hand he held something, and then in the glare of the searchlight I saw it: Androsa's snubnose .38.

He came up to me, almost sauntering, the damp bulk of him sliding across my deck.

"I am wondering, Capitán MacMorgan, why you

thought it necessary to come to Cuba with such a weapon," he said, holding the handgun up for my inspection.

And I was about to give the weak explanation that I used it for sharks, when Androsa cut in, speaking in fast Spanish—too fast for me to understand.

Lobo tilted his head, listening, seemingly entertained by what she had to tell him. When she was finished, he turned to me. "*Capitán*, do you know what this woman says? She says that she brought this little gun because she did not trust you."

I tried to look shocked. "What?"

He chuckled; a lecherous laugh. "But I think you are not the kind of man to remain a stranger to any woman, eh?"

I still had my arm around Androsa's shoulder. His inference was obvious. I shrugged and said nothing.

Waving his hand, Lobo ordered his men back aboard the gunboat. And he was about to step across himself when Zapata, looking meaner than ever, stopped him with a harsh burst of Spanish. Lobo answered briefly, then waited stoically while his fellow officer let go with another emotional tirade.

Captain Lobo turned back to me, saying, "My friend here says that I have been remiss in my search."

"Is that so?"

"Perhaps. He says that we did not look up on your flybridge."

I sighed, relieved—but tried not to show it. And then: "He says that I also failed to check your . . . *individuo* . . . the clothes on your back, eh?"

I lifted my hands theatrically. "The body is in my back pocket, Captain. I must confess."

Dry laugh without humor. Lobo didn't like jokers. "No, of course not." He motioned with the woman's revolver. "But you might have another of these, yes?"

"No, but you're welcome to look."

While a soldier scampered up the ladder to have a look around the flybridge, Lobo frisked me. His hands were fat, stubby, and they pounded down my sides like little bricks.

"Convinced?"

"*Sí!* For now."

I wanted to do something, anything, to make them forget about searching the woman.

But it was too late. Zapata was already vectoring in on her, giving her orders in sharp Spanish. I felt all eyes turn toward the woman. She was beautiful, unbelievably so, and all of the soldiers wanted to see what she wore beneath the robe.

She backed away from Zapata, clutching the bulky cloak around her, moving toward me instinctively.

"You're not going to let that creep take her clothes off, are you? She's naked underneath—"

Lobo punched me solidly in the stomach with his elbow, and I had to grit my teeth to keep from showing any pain. "You must learn, gringo, to show proper respect for a Cuban officer." He never took his eyes off the woman as he spoke.

So it was show time. It had been a long night for Castro's toy troops. They had gunned down an unarmed man and had worn themselves out searching for the corpse. Now it was time for a little recreation. Time to force the pretty senorita to strip.

Right.

She bumped into me and stopped. End of the trail. Zapata came up, standing toe to toe with her. He grabbed the lapel of robe and she knocked his hand away.

The soldiers on the gunboat roared with laughter. See the beautiful woman fight the big strong *capitán!*

So the audience was with us, not him. It might make a difference. I might be able to make a move, and they might laugh instead of shoot, and . . .

Maybe hell.

Zapata was yelling at Androsa, now—furious. He was tired of being made a fool of. He kept nodding at me as he spoke, and it became clear what he was accusing her of—being a whore for the big blond gringo. It was the old sexual taboo, a light-skinned person sexually intimate with the darker-skinned. And that seemed to make him madder than anything.

This Zapata was a jerk, all right.

And I prayed the opportunity would come for me to even the score.

Tired of having his orders scorned, he grabbed the woman and ripped the robe back. And just as quickly, she pulled it tightly around her and, with her free left hand, slapped him a loud stinger across the face.

More laughter from the gunboat.

"Puta!" he screamed. His face was crimson from the slap. He touched the swelling area, hesitated, then slapped her in return, jerking her head back. I caught her in my arms.

It was time to make my move; to take care of Zapata before he forced the robe open and saw the bloodstain. And I knew what I was going to do. Cold-cock the skinny bastard, then assume the roll of the gringo clown, hoping the soldier-audience would laugh instead of shoot—

But I didn't have time to try it. With a low animal screech, she launched herself at Zapata, using hands and fingernails at his face, backing him up. Then she brought that left hand of hers from waist high in a sizzling uppercut. Zapata was in the absolute worst position for it. He was bent at the waist, head down, trying to protect his eyes.

So the lancing fist caught him flush on his bird nose. There was a surprisingly loud *thwack*, an explosion of cartilage and blood, and it sent him wheeling backward.

And he didn't have far to go.

The transom caught him thigh-high, and he went tumbling ass-end first into the black water.

There was a tense moment; a moment of indecision for the soldiers. And then Lobo led the way. His laughter—loud and genuine—detonated the glee of the others. They roared in spasms, holding their stomachs, pounding the deck of the gunboat. By the time they had regained sufficient control to remember their fallen captain, he had floundered his way

back to the surface. He screamed threats at the world.
He singled the woman out again and again, pointing
dreadful promises at her with his index finger.

And he meant every one of them.

When the gunboat finally rumbled away, I pulled
the woman close to me. She was shivering noticeably.

"We're going to have to watch out for that one
from now on," I said.

"Yes, I know. I was probably very stupid." Her
dark eyes were glazed with the shock of what she
had done; of how close we both had come to capture.

"It wasn't stupid," I said. "In fact, I was going to
punch him if you didn't. It was our only chance."

She said nothing, just leaned there trembling
against me; the shock coming in low swells, flowing
through her body. "Hey," I said. "It's over. You can
relax now."

She slid around so that she faced me, her arms
around me, small hands low on the base of my back.
A satin wisp of hair covered her left eye. I reached
down, brushed it away, and when I did she touched
my hand with her lips.

"There's only one way I can relax now, Dusky."

Her lips were moist, slightly parted, and the mahogany eyes seemed to bore into mine. "Please,
Dusky. I . . . I don't want to be alone tonight. Not
down there. Not where he . . ."

I kissed her gently, a searching kiss, asking her if
she wanted only companionship, to be held—or
more. Her mouth opened, tongue communicating
without words. Her long legs pressed, then curled

around mine, and I lifted her up into my arms, still caressing her lips with mine. I said her name softly, a whisper: "Androsa Santarun. You are quite a woman, Androsa Santarun."

Her response was a weary smile. She frowned for a moment, as if trying to remember something, and then I heard her words like an echo of my own. "Yes," she said. "I'm something. I'm a real goddam ace. . . ."

12

The next morning, several hours before the radio informed Androsa that immigration authorities wanted to see her in Havana, I spent the glowing dusky dawn time alone engaged in the idle musings of a man who has seen his life of the-straight-and-narrow dissolve into a strange existence of cricks, crinks, and clashes in the fast lane.

It was an airy blue morning. Molten gold in the east: the sun spinning hard toward a billion tiny lives in the western hemisphere.

That's you, MacMorgan. One rogue speck in the giant montage of living cells. See yourself? That's right. Get out the big microscope. . . .

A brash night wind had come down out of the mountains of Mesa de Mariel and blown the factory smog away. It cleaned the air and made the harbor seem almost pristine. Even the rattiest among the thousands of American boats in the harbor looked clean and white in that morning light, and you could see the little thatched-roof village on the plateau of distant cane fields plainly.

It was a good morning for breaking rules, so I cracked a rare bottle of Heineken dark and sipped at it while I dressed. Put on clean khaki fishing shorts, soft and stained with the blood of many good fish. Add the old leather belt with the brass anchor, strap on the Gerber knife in its oil-blackened case, and, just for the hell of it, check the blade. Sharp enough to shave blond hair off the left arm—but it could be sharper. A good way to spend the morning: sip at the beer, work on the knife with honing oil and ceramic stone and watch the morning filter across Cuban landscape.

I pulled on a white cotton shirt, then poked my head into the veeing of master berth.

Androsa was asleep. Her hair fanned out beneath her head like a black satin pillow, and her nose flared slightly with every inhalation. The white sheet was pulled up just over her pelvis, and the outline of hips was a shadowed curve with the soft lift of inner thigh tapering toward long legs. Her thin ribs were alternately visible and invisible with every breath, and her right arm curved up under the delicate chin, flattening the right breast, showing only a portion of the dark-brown aureola of nipple.

Funny how intimate contact sharpens your attention, focuses your eyes. You notice the little anatomical variants that you did not see before.

There was a tiny white fingernail of scar below her

left cheek. And just the slightest hint of lines at the corner of her eyes, sun-furrowed. Confident of her natural beauty, she wore no makeup and did not employ the little cosmetic tricks most women use. So her eyebrows were in light disarray, and her lips were pale, without lipstick. Her skin was the color of sandalwood, sun-darkened, with thin white bikini marks around her breasts.

Gently, I kissed her on the forehead.

She stirred, flinched, dreaming. . . .

"Dusky . . . ?"

"Hum . . . ?"

"Dusky . . ."

"Go back to sleep, lady."

I went topside with knife and stone and oil can, dark beer cold in my hand.

People were beginning to stir on nearby boats. Men in underwear came out onto their morning decks, hacked, spit, stretched. In the freshening wind was the smell of bacon frying, and the diesel odor of the harbor. Over on the beach by the little military outpost, the guard had been doubled. Cuban soldiers in their baggy uniforms walked the beach, urging their German shepherds to find the body that could never be found.

So you did it, MacMorgan. You outfoxed the foxes. And how many other bodies have you had to hide in your lifetime? Just those two? Right. The first, a North Vietnamese, had been easy. You only needed to buy a few extra hours to get your men out. So who would think of looking in the highest branches of an avocado tree for a point guard? The second had been tougher—even tougher than the one last night. A Russian special forces ace who had been sent out for one reason, and one reason only— to nail the Navy SEAL who had the disconcerting ability to drift jungle rivers at night, make silent one-man assaults on important Commie strongholds, then disappear leaving only the corpses of officers and double agents in his path, arrow holes or knife smiles in each and every one. Yes, the body of the Russian had been the hardest to hide because you could not afford to let him ever be found—not there, not where he had finally walked into your trap. Even if it meant the grizzly business the job demanded, the one and only way to strike him and his remains from the face of the earth for ever and ever . . .

Remembering, I felt the revulsion low in my stomach, and then I took a sip of the cold dark beer, feeling the memory wash away like phlegm.

A good morning for idle musing—but not about that.

So I worked at the knife, oiling the blade and carving at the whetstone. And I thought about how it had been with the woman.

Some woman.

Some lover.

Androsa Santarun was, in love, much the same as she was in life: straightforward, without guile, a person of strength who knew what she wanted. But all of these qualities were shaded with a gentleness and the hint of vulnerability that made her as passionate about pleasing as she was passionate about her wanting.

I had steered her down into the cabin, both hands on her frail shoulders, feeling her trembling beneath my touch. The main cabin lamp was on, throwing a glaze of yellow light across the big vee-berth. And when I reached to switch it off, she had stopped my hand.

"I . . . leave it on. Please, I want to see . . ."

The robe fell off her shoulders, and she turned to me in the golden light, nipples erect beneath a thin fabric of T-shirt, hips moving with the motion of the first long kiss.

"You're sure," I said, doubtful even then of the wisdom of changing our relationship so irreversibly.

And she had pulled my mouth back down to hers. "Yes. I've never been so sure about anything."

There was a desperate, feverish quality to our first long joining; a surge of total wanting that was at once both exciting and troubling. It pulled at my mind for a time—until I remembered the source of it; something I had read. During the bombing of London in World War II, the underground shelters had spawned a whole new race of children; some legitimate, most not. People of that time had written about the increased sexuality of love during the bombings— like some biological drive to procreate on the razor's edge of death.

And, strangely, that's the way it was with Androsa; as if some blackness watched from outside, waiting only until we had finished our feverish coupling to strike.

"Is this all right . . . ?"

"Oh Dusky, oh yes, yes, yes—but turn . . . turn around so that I can . . ."

It was a night of distilled wanting, of concentrated emotion pouring from the two of us; sometimes gentle, sometimes savage, always churning toward the timeless merging into oneness that left the strangers—which we were—far behind.

"Oh Dusky, you are so . . ."

"You don't have to say anything, Androsa. But just for the record, you are too."

And later, after our voracious hunger had been temporarily satiated, we talked.

Or, more correctly, she talked. She told me of her difficult adjustment to American life, of her college years, and of the husband she had loved so much and wanted everything for, only to see all hopes destroyed by some drunken driver who did not notice the jogger one sunlit Sunday afternoon.

But mostly, she talked of her childhood in Cuba.

"I was born on a large island south of the mainland," she told me, her soft weight stretched out on top of me, breasts mashed firm and flat against my chest.

"The Isle of Pines?"

"Yes! Isla de Pinos—do you know it?"

"Not well. You tell me about it."

She rolled off me, holding me across the chest, speaking softly into my ear. "As a child, I thought it the most beautiful place in the world. We lived in a little village in a harbor called Ensenada de Siguanea, and the water was very clear, and even as a child I would swim out to watch the fish that lived around the coral. I think that we were probably very poor, because our house had only two rooms and the roof was made of thatch. But we always had plenty of food, and bananas and oranges grew outside, and there were always fish and rice and mangos."

"You're making me hungry." I reached over and brushed hair from her face. "Did you have any brothers or sisters?"

She hesitated for a moment. "Yes. A half brother. And such a good brother, Alvino. He was only two years older, but even then he spoiled me."

"Hum, you don't taste spoiled. So is your brother in America now? Why didn't he come back to Mariel for your father?"

I felt her tense momentarily. "My brother . . . my brother is dead. Castro's people murdered him. Like animals, they killed him."

"So you have only your mother now?"

"And my father."

I expected the tension to ease out of her, but it didn't. The reserves were up again. I had planned on following her lead; hoping she would tell me the truth about her mission so that I could tell her the truth about mine. Instead, she evaded questions about her home life, her occupation, and fell into a brief lie about the man we had come to get, her fictional father.

"I don't remember much about him. Only that he was very large and smelled of tobacco, and he was a soldier. I remember that he frightened me. And that he was always away."

"Was it your father who taught you how to shoot?"

"What? Oh, yes—in a way. He was not home that much. Even so, he is my father, and I am dedicated to him in my own way. We are of the same blood, you see. To a Cuban, that means everything."

"Your father is very lucky to have a daughter like you."

She touched my lips with her fingertip, silencing me.

"Please," she said. "No more talk. We will have many days to talk." She rolled back on me, kissing my chest, my stomach, sliding downward. "This is the time for loving. Like before, only . . ."

"Only what, lady."

She smiled, almost blushing. "Only even harder. Much harder. I am a strong woman, Mr. Dusky MacMorgan. You cannot break me. . . ."

So I sat in the starboard fighting chair, swiveling back and forth idly, working at the knife. The blade was looking good: only two or three burrs from fishbone, and the ceramic stone was working them out nicely. Once I had loaned the knife to a tourist fisherman down at the docks. He was having trouble getting the heads off some small barracuda he had caught, and was just about ready to toss his frail Sears fillet knife into the water when I came along. It seemed like a harmless request, so I unsheathed the Gerber for him, and went about my business aboard *Sniper*. When I returned to the cleaning table, the man was gone. Someone said he had headed up to the marina. I went after him on a dead run. And I got there just in time. He had the grinding wheel going and was just about to "resharpen" my knife to "thank me" for the loan.

If it hadn't been such an honest effort to do me a favor, I would have dropped him in his tracks. Even so, he looked a little taken aback by the lecture I gave him. You don't use a grinding wheel on a fine knife, ever, ever, ever, buddy. It's like trying to clean a handgun by throwing it in the washing machine. . . .

I checked the blade on my arm again. Blond hair came off as readily as if the folding knife were one of those twin-blade razors. I folded it, housed it back on my belt, then went below to start breakfast for the woman.

I cracked six eggs, stirred them into a pan, added chopped onion and a touch of A&B hot sauce. By the time the omelet was ready for cheese and a careful fold, Androsa came out of the master berth, head tilted, combing her long black hair with a brush.

"Food's almost ready."

"Hum. Good."

I listened carefully for any sign of new reserve in her voice. If there was to be an awkward time, this would be it. It is the most modern of afflictions: how do total strangers deal with each other after they have just shared the most intimate of experiences?

There is the forced hilarity or the coy shyness, or the manufactured innocence of "Gee, did it really happen, because I'm normally not like that."

But Androsa Santarun displayed nothing but affection and a wry sense of humor. She strolled by me, still combing her hair, then reached over and gave me a surprise kiss on the lips.

"Smells good," she said.

"And suddenly I'm not very hungry."

She slapped at me. "After . . . our last time, you swore you wouldn't have any energy for a week!"

"You know how we gringos love to lie."

She plopped herself down at the little booth. She wore dark-blue Dolphin running shorts and a baggy shirt, sleeves folded up to her elbows. "Well, at least feed me first. I might be skinny, but this Hispanic body of mine won't run on air. And, if you don't mind, I'll take a small glass of that dark beer you just opened for yourself."

It was a good day, a rare day filled with sun and jokes and love and tanning oil measured out by the handfuls on naked bodies; a day marred only by our anchorage in that dismal harbor with its acid smog and the atmosphere of desperation perpetuated by the loud amplified drone of the Cubans' calling various boats to Pier Three where they would be loaded with their human cargo.

One time I caught the sadness in Androsa's eyes as she listened to it.

"Were they calling us?"

She shook her head, startled out of whatever it was

she was thinking about. "No, not yet. But you never know. I guess we should keep the radio on just in case."

I should never have done it; never let her turn on that static reminder of why we had come: VHF 16 with its endless Spanish dialogue of anger and desperation, interrupted by the Castro regime every four hours to list the boats that were about to be loaded. But it happens that way sometimes. All your instincts tell you no while your reason thinks it knows better.

I should have followed my instincts.

But I didn't. And there was no way of knowing that the radio call would mean the loss of the woman I was just learning to love. . . .

13

The call came at about four p.m.

They must have repeated it a couple of times, because it took a while for even Androsa to hear it. But there it was: blasts of static, and then, *"Atención, atención—embarcación* Sniper."

We were stretched out on the high privacy of the flybridge, both of us stripped to the waist, baking in the sun. She used my stomach as a cushion for her head. I used one of the heavy commercial-grade life jackets. We had spent most of the afternoon like that. I had brought up a small cooler filled with ice to keep the beer and a few cans of fruit juice cold. It was a good place to talk, to touch occasionally, and to read. I was rereading Peter Matthiessen's very fine book *Snow Leopard*, and I had entrusted Androsa with one of my favorite and very finest books: the 1912 first edition of H.M. Tomlinson's *The Sea and the Jungle*. It is a rare book and, like the *Snow Leopard*, the kind you want to share only with the rarest of people. I had offered her first Papa's *The Old Man and the Sea*, but she had declined immediately, saying that it always made her cry—not only the story but because he had captured Cuba the way she remembered it as a child. So, before placing it securely back in the big watertight ammo box which guarded my ship's library, I opened the front cover and read the loved inscription for the thousandth time: *This is the best I have to offer, Old Timer. And it's yours.*

It was a good way to spend the afternoon. Fine books. Cold beer. Warm sun. Time enough for Androsa to write a letter or two. And anticipation of the evening's love. I had made up my mind to corner her that night; to work my way into her confidence and then tell her exactly what *both* our jobs were in Mariel Harbor.

And to try to convince her that our jobs were over.

Fact: *Storm Nest*, the trawler which had transported the three CIA agents to Cuba, had been found bullet-riddled in American waters. True, the agents were not aboard—but neither was General Halcón, the Cuban crossover. And common sense dictated that, if someone was going to steal the boat and try the crossing, he, as the director of security in Mariel, would certainly have the first opportunity.

But he wasn't on the boat. Why? According to Norm Fizer, things were getting hot for the Hawk.

Maybe things got too hot. Maybe Castro and his people put two and two together and decided that

Halcón was a bad apple—and gave him a carbine trial. So, who was left to rescue?

Fact: One of the CIA agents, Ovillo Gomez, was now one very dead man, resting thirty feet beneath water and mud and my very own *Sniper*. If he and his two friends had really set out to bump off Castro, what in the hell was he doing trying to swim to my boat? No, it seemed more likely that they had, indeed, been snatched by Castro's people. But how had Gomez found out that Androsa Santarun was on my boat? Coincidence, maybe . . . yeah, coincidence.

Bullshit, MacMorgan. You're supposed to be the big man who prides himself on his personal honesty. Now you're trying to conjure up some pretty damn weak evidence to convince yourself that you should hustle that pretty woman back to Key West, out of harm's way. A day ago it didn't make any difference to you—you told yourself that if she wanted to bait the tiger trap, it was her decision. Now, after sharing her bed, you're suddenly hell-bent on calling the whole thing off. You know this mission hasn't been resolved. Too many missing links. Too many abstract facts that don't add up. And if you do convince yourself, you can bet that one Stormin' Norman Fizer is going to tell you in pretty rough language just what a fool you've been once you do make it back to Key West. . . .

So I was locked in that personal struggle when the VHF beckoned.

Androsa lifted her head off my stomach. "Did you hear that?" And then: "They're calling us, Dusky."

She hurried down the ladder below. I heard the conversation, muffled, fast, and very damn short. When she was finished, she poked her head up over the flybridge deck.

"So what's up, lady?"

"Nothing important. I'm supposed to go into Havana and use the government phone so I can call my father and apprise him of the situation."

She was very calm and cool; but it was a business-like cool. And I knew that she wasn't telling me the whole truth.

"You're sure he really wants to go to America? Maybe he's just clam-happy over here working for the dream of socialism?"

She smiled at me and winked. "Maybe. But I have to try. I'm going to change and flag down one of those government taxi boats that keep going by. Apparently there are a few *tiendas* up harbor at Pier Two where they sell beer and food and stuff, and a government bus leaves there every hour for some hotel—I think it was called the Triton—where there are phones and the immigration people have offices."

"So I'll just slip into my good shirt and pants and play escort—"

"No!" The firmness with which she said it surprised even her. "I mean, I'd feel terrible if you went off and left your boat unguarded and something happened to it."

"Are you still trying to give orders?"

She reached out and ran her short fingernails down

my thigh. "For now. How about it, ya big lug? Stay here and mind the store while I go into the city for an hour or so. Believe me, I'll hurry right back."

She said it like some peroxide blonde in a 1930 detective film, and I had to laugh.

"You play a bad Harlow with that Spanish accent of yours."

She wiggled her finger, telling me to come to her. When I did, she kissed me lightly, then harder, and even the breaking away held promise. "Keep that for me until I get back, okay?"

"It's a tough job, but somebody has to do it."

She smiled, cupping my chin in her small hand. "You're something special, Dusky MacMorgan. Very special."

"And so are you, lady. So are you. . . ."

The moment her taxi boat disappeared behind the first shrimp trawler, I started looking for a taxi of my own. She had left in an old confiscated Woodson trihull painted bright red with a muscular Cuban at the wheel. He wore small black bikini trunks, and he gave me a dirty leer as I waved goodbye to Androsa.

That's right, fella. She's mine. And don't forget it.

By the time I'd flagged down a boat, she was half-way across the harbor, and I knew I'd have to hurry to catch her. When the skiff pulled up, I thought about locking *Sniper*—then decided that would probably be the worst thing to do. If the Cubans wanted to search her badly enough, they'd just bust in to do

it. So, still zipping up my pants and trying to slide
into my Topsiders, I swung down onto the waiting
skiff.

There were two men aboard. One was obviously
the government driver. He wore the standard baggy
green pants, cut off at the cuffs instead of hemmed.
He was about forty, haggard and unshaven, and a
stub of cigarette butt grew from the corner of his
mouth. He looked bored and uncommunicative.

"Quanto dinero?" I asked him.

He held up a spread palm. Five bucks, American.
I shoved a ten at him. *"Tu hablas inglés?"*

He shook his head. I got the feeling that if he did
speak English he wasn't about to let me know it. I
slapped my hand on the gunwall of the skiff.

"Damn!"

I could reach into my memory and give him
enough bad Spanish to make him understand I
wanted to go to Pier Two, but what if the woman's
skiff veered off, made an earlier stop? Shoving the
driver aside and taking control of the boat might
make me seem a bad risk in the eyes of Captain
Lobo. And I couldn't afford to let him become any
more suspicious of me.

"Do you need some help there, Yank?"

For the first time, I noticed the second man in the
boat. He wasn't Cuban—no doubt about that. He was
a little younger than I, in his early thirties, and he
had copper-colored hair and a bright-red beard. The
size of him and the musculature made me think of
the Vikings: just under six feet tall, 190 pounds,

maybe, with the shoulders of a wrestler. He had the gnomish face of a Scandinavian seaman, and an accent that seemed to be a mixture of heavy Irish and light British. His thighs were thick, heavily muscled beneath cutoff shorts, and he wore a black T-shirt inscribed: *Bodden Town Dive Trips.*

"If you speak Spanish, and you've got some spare time, I can use all the help you can offer," I said.

He grinned and stuck out his hand. "Westy is me name. Westy O'Davis. And I do speak Spanish—bloody bad Spanish, but Cubans speak the worst kind of Spanish, so they understand mine jest fine. So what kin' I do for ya, Yank?"

Roughly, I explained the situation to him after introducing myself. There were plenty of holes in my story, but he seemed to sense it wouldn't do to ask questions.

"So you want ta follow the lady, but you don't want ta catch her—that about right?"

"Pretty much."

He looked amused, his left hand tugging at the red beard. He thought for a moment, then nodded his assent. "So be it! No, don't thank me. It's yerself who are favoring me. After twenty-two days in this hellhole of a harbor, it's a pleasure to have the company of an American. I'm a one who trusts his instincts, and me instincts say yer okay, Yank. So let me have a word with this mutton-headed driver and we'll be on our way. Right!"

It was more argument than conversation. Westy O'Davis kept his hands on his hips, bent slightly at

the waist, nose aimed right at the nose of the government boat driver. Every time the driver tried to
speak, the stocky Irishman shoved loud Spanish into
his face, refusing to allow his demands to be chal-
lenged. Finally, the driver relented, worn down and
taciturn.

"Done!" said O'Davis, swinging toward me, smiling. "Didn't tell 'em we wanted to follow a boat. Jes
tol' 'em we wanted to travel 'round the harbor a
bit—and that we would tell him where to go. These
reds are suspicious people; didn't figure it would do
to tell 'em we was shadowin' a lady."

"Perfect," I said. "I appreciate it. Now look, I'm
not keeping you from some kind of business, am I?
I know you're not riding around in a government
taxi boat for your health—"

He held up his hand, the gesture implying the un-
importance of his own plans. "Do you see that big
black wind ship over there a piece?"

I did. And it wasn't the first time I had noticed
her. She was a beauty: a gaff-rigged schooner, taller
aft mast made of stout golden pine, the foremast flying the blue British ensign with the flag badge of the
islands in the center.

"You're from the Caymans?"

He nodded. "And she's my pride and joy. The only
time she and myself part normally is when I go tarpon guiding in the spring up to Boca Grande, Florida, in your own U.S.A. to make a few extra for her
and me own pocket. But after three weeks aboard
listenin' to that bloody loud Spanish, an' smellin' the

foul smell of me own self, I'm about to go ravin' looney." He spread his arms. "So you see, Yank, I'm a takin' you under me wing outta graditude. One scarred-up old seaman to another in a harbor full of fools. How 'bout it?" He spit in his palm, offered his hand, and I took it.

"My pleasure," I said.

And I meant it. I had seen it before in foreign lands. Friendships among strangers are struck up with no better criterion than a lost look or the color of your hair. In a country of aliens and alien ideology, kindred spirits come together as if drawn by magnets. And surprisingly, the friendships usually continue long afterward. Joined in the common bond of circumstance, all the bullshit social hurdles fall away and you are left with an honesty that demands either mutual loyalty or mutual hatred. And with this stocky Irishman, I knew it would be mutual loyalty. I also suspected that, no matter what, I would have met Westy O'Davis sooner or later. Because that's the way things happen in a place like Mariel Harbor.

I kept a close eye on the bright-red Woodson. And so did he.

"Yank, I believe yer lady friend is headed for the Love Boat."

"The Love what?"

He chuckled. "That bugger Castro has thought of jest about every way possible to make money in this hellhole. It's that medium-tonnage ocean liner over there—the *Comandante Pinares*. Folks 'round here call it the Love Boat 'cause there's whiskey an' food—an'

women too, if you've money enough." He tapped
the driver on the shoulder and told him where we
wanted to go. The driver acted as if it took every
ounce of his strength to force the skiff onto plane,
the little Russian outboard belching oil as we went.
It was a good half mile to the liner, and as we pounded
along Westy O'Davis tried to replace my growing anxi-
ety with conversation. He told me how, as a kid of
sixteen, he had shipped out of Dun Laoghaire on Ireland's east coast on a Honduran freighter. On the
freighter he had learned two things: how to speak
Spanish, and never to trust any vessel with a Liberian
registry, Honduran or otherwise. Or, as he put it,
"Them bloody Africans would register a bamboo raft
as a thousand-ton oil tanker if you paid the bribe in
cash!" He had jumped ship off Cayman Brac, swum
to shore, then worked his way to Grand Cayman,
where a friendly Englishman helped him get a work
permit from Government House. In time, he got a job
guiding scuba-diving trips in Bodden Town, and an
American had talked him into going to America to run
his big Chris-Craft as a tarpon boat in Boca Grande
during the big spring run. With the money he had
saved, he made a down payment on his black schooner. And this Cuban trip would pay it off.

"And no island woman snapped you up during
all that time," I said, teasing him.

The look which came into his eyes was a stoicism
underlined with the tragic. "Aye, one did. But she's
gone now."

I didn't press for an explanation.

The *Comandante Pinares* was about three hundred feet of antiquated liner painted a shoddy white, bottom-fouled, anchored solidly fore and aft. Floating aluminum docks crushed up against the hulls, and the docks were surrounded by small boats, loading and unloading. Harsh Latin music was being piped around the crowded decks through tinny speakers, and soldiers and plainclothesmen stood conspicuously at the boarding ladders.

"What's th' matter, Yank? You look troubled."

"I can't understand why she came here. She told me she was going to a place called Pier Two. She was supposed to catch a bus there and talk to the immigration authorities in Havana."

He slapped me on the shoulder. "You never kin figure 'em out, mate—I've tried. But if it'll ease your mind any, there's immigration people here, too. Upper deck, where you see that line o' people. Maybe she jes' changed her mind."

The red-hulled Woodson was tethered up at the floating docks, the muscular taxi pilot still aboard, but Androsa was nowhere in sight. So now what? Board the liner and take the chance of letting Androsa know that I was following her? Why not? I had a right to be concerned. If she saw me, I'd play the roll of the overprotective lover. It couldn't hurt. No way.

Right.

"What's the plan, mate?" Westy looked at me expectantly.

"The plan, my new friend, is for you to go on about your business. It's just a hunch, but I think my lady friend might be in a little trouble. And I'd hate for you to get involved—"

"Horsefeathers!" He looked genuinely offended. "Was it not I meself who spit in me palm and offered you me own hand? Sure it was. Blast your trouble!" He grinned at me. "Besides, I can't very well abandon a mate with a fine name like MacMorgan, now, could I—Yank or not."

"Okay, okay—you can tag along on one condition."

He spread his arms in grand gesture. "You've only to name it."

"If it looks like there's going to be any rough stuff, you get your ass out of there quick."

"Mush, mush—and do I look like a fool? A course I will, a course I will. I swear it on the grave of me own dead mother."

When our driver finally managed to nose up to the crowded docks, I jumped out and pulled O'Davis up behind me. He was surprisingly nimble for his size. Before we headed up the ladder to the main deck, he turned and wagged his finger at our Cuban driver, railing at him in a guttural Spanish.

"What were you lecturing him about?"

"No lecture, Yank. Convinced him to stay until we came back out."

"I hate to be a spoilsport, but these Castro Cubans aren't known for keeping their promises."

Westy O'Davis gave me a conspirator's wink. "This one will. I told him you were a very important man, mate. Had to lie a wee bit—told him you were a Russian adviser. Believed me, too—imagine that."

14

The bar of the *Comandante Pinares* was long and narrow, with the obligatory mirror behind the sparse liquor stock and a floor made of aluminum sheeting that seemed to bow with each step. Booths along the outer bulkhead were packed with Cuban-Americans busy with plates of black beans and yellow rice. Frail waiters dressed in white shirts and black ties moved sluggishly through the noise and smoke. There were a couple of stools open at the bar, so my red-bearded friend and I took a seat and ordered beer.

Westy lifted his eyebrows, questioning me. I shook my head. "She's not in here," I said.

It was a Czechoslovakian beer served in big dark bottles, and the entire head when poured consisted of about four massive bubbles which suggested, it seemed, that the brewer had included dishwater in his recipe.

But it was good beer, strong and cold, and Westy

did quick justice to it and ordered more. When it came, he poured his glass full, tasted it experimentally, and clicked his tongue, pleased.

He said, "Nothin' like that first taste of beer, eh, mate?"

"It does rank right up there."

He swiveled on his stool, toying with the glass. He had a big blunt ruddy face, a trace of scar between cheek and Gaelic nose, and bright-blue eyes that were easy to read.

"Having some second thoughts there, O'Davis?"

He squenched up one eye mischievously. "Hah! Yank, once me mind's made up, I've made up me mind." He paused for a moment, and then: "I've sailed most a the world, spent half me life in foreign ports. Seen a lotta boatmen white and otherwise and I've learned to know the ones that aren't worth a flip and the ones that are, and—well, I give you me hand, didn't I?"

"But you've been thinking," I added.

"Sure I've been a-thinkin'. I've been a-sittin' here wondering how important that lady is that we're chasin'. Is she your wife or your wench or jest a charter or what?"

"Just a very important person, you might say, O'Davis." I felt him eyeing me, and I had to grin. "Okay, okay," I said. "I'm being secretive. But there's a reason. Tell you what—next time you're in the States, come to Key West. You can stay with me for a couple of weeks and we'll fish and drink beer all day and tell tall tales. And I'll give you the whole story. But for now it has to be my way."

"And don't be a-thinkin' I won't take you up on that kind offer. You have the look of the mystery about you, brother MacMorgan, and a very interestin' story it will be, no doubt."

"And you have the look of one very nosy Irishman, O'Davis."

He cackled at that. "Sure an' it's true, true! But sittin' here among these wolves and mother dogs, who else do you have to trust?"

As we sat there, O'Davis told me all he knew about the layout of the *Pinares*. Just aft of the bar was a little souvenir shop where they sold green cigars and T-shirts. Outside and up the stairs was the immigration office and, cabined beside that, a larger room where, for a price, there were prostitutes and gambling.

"What about below?"

He shook his head. "Never been down there—an' I've been jest about everyplace an outsider can go in me three weeks here."

I raised my eyebrows.

"An' what does that mean, Yank?"

"It means you should stay here while I have a look around."

"But ya canna go strollin' down inta the belly of the ship like ya own the place. There's guards, mate. I've seen 'em me own self. Two of 'em above an' God knows how many below."

"All I can do is try. I don't want to lose that woman."

There was a kind sympathy in his blue eyes. "Ya talk like a man who's lost a woman before."

"And you talk like a man who knows what that means," I said.

When I turned to go, he grabbed my shoulder. "Hold on there, now. You'll be needin' a diversion, I'm thinkin'."

"Or maybe just a lost look. You know how easily us stupid Americans get lost."

"But a diversion would be a fair sight better." He held up his finger as if lecturing. "Have you ever noticed, Yank, what a hot-blooded people these Cubans be? Fine folk, mostly—but hot-blooded." He nodded toward two men sitting on stools down from ours. They were young, wore T-shirts, and both had tattoos. "Now take those two fellas. I'd be willin' to bet me last Cayman dollar, picture of the Queen an' all, that if I was to suggest to one that the other told me his sister was a *putana*, why I bet there would be one hell of a diversion."

"Don't try it, O'Davis—"

But it was too late. He was already stretched out over the counter laughing like a drunk, barking Spanish at the two men in his Irish brogue. It didn't take long for them to react. While the one glowered at O'Davis, the other stood up and dumped beer on his former friend, yelling challenges. The other answered with a roundhouse right that sent chin and body crashing into the next table. When the guards rushed in to break it up, people started shoving and more fights broke out. Pretty soon the narrow bar of the *Comandante Pinares* was, indeed, one hell of a diversion.

Westy O'Davis picked his beer up gingerly, careful lest it be spilled by the combatants, then backed away, nudging me ahead of him.

"Do ya see what I mean, friend MacMorgan?" he said in a silly half-whisper. "Hot-blooded!"

"O'Davis, you fool, you swore to me on your mother's grave that you wouldn't get involved in any rough stuff."

"Ah, 'deed I did, 'deed I did." Then he glanced at me with a sly look. "Funny thing about me mother's grave—it's empty, it is. The old girl runs a little pub in Kilcullen outside Kildare. Last I heard, she was still arm 'rasslin' the farm lads for bottles o' port." He tapped me on the shoulder. "Here they come, Yank—the guards from the bowels o' the ship. Now's the time to make yer move. I'm thinkin' I'll jest stay up here and enjoy the spectacle."

The guards came rushing past us, automatic weapons slung on slings over their shoulders. They carried green aerosol cans—probably Mace.

In long confident strides, hands in pockets, I moved down the hallway and took the aluminum steps two at a time. The main corridor belowdeck was tiled with mud-colored linoleum, and the bulkheads were painted gray. I had to make a decision:

aft or forward? The engine rooms would be aft. And
the crew quarters. I took a chance and headed toward
the bow.

I had pressed my ear against the hatchways of
three cabins before I finally heard the voices.

Strident Spanish. The imperious voice of a man
followed by the muffled replies of a woman. It was
no ordinary conversation. The male voice was demanding, threatening, the woman's was controlled
but edged with underlying emotion.

I knew the voice. I had heard it whisper my name
over and over the night before.

It was the voice of Androsa Santarun.

I fought off the urge to force my way into the
room, kick ass and take names later. This was no
place for a rescue attempt. The ship was crawling
with guards. It was still daylight. And even if I did
get the woman and make it out, there was no way
of getting us back to *Sniper.* The government boat
pilot might believe me to be Russian, but there was
no way he'd play cat and mouse with his own people. Besides, there was still the off chance—however
slight—that this was some kind of standard immigration interrogation.

There was no absolute proof that Androsa had
been kidnapped.

Not yet, anyway.

I leaned against the door, straining to hear. As
shoddy as the ship was, the bulkheads were solid
and thick, and I could catch only snatches of the
man's voice. It was the heavy growl of someone used

to authority: flat, demanding, unyielding. I picked up only a few words.

"*. . . espia . . . nombres . . .*"

Nombres was Spanish for "names." And it was easy enough to figure out what *espia* meant.

They had her. No doubt about that now. And I knew what the fate of a beautiful American spy woman would be in the hands of the Castro Cubans. Last night, after our lovemaking, she had whispered to me that I had been her first since the death of her husband. And it had been something good for her; something desperately important and special. Thinking about what the soldiers would do to her after they had reamed every bit of useful information out of her made my stomach roll.

Hang on, good lady. Don't give up. Your luck hasn't run out yet. . . .

The sound of footsteps jerked me from my thoughts. Coming down the aluminum stairs. Heavy steps, one man in a hurry. Hard-bottomed shoes. Military shoes.

It was a long corridor. Before me lay a dead end. Behind, toward the stairs, was the only hope of a hiding place—a narrow offshoot from the main hallway which ended, probably, in a small room. I gauged the sound of the footsteps, wondering if I had time to make it to the intersecting hall. And knew, then, that I didn't.

First the shadow moved around the corner, then the man himself—a burly Cuban soldier with an AK-47 in hand. He was light-skinned and broad-faced with pockmarks and a mustache. He looked at me, surprised. And I knew I had only one chance. I lifted my arms, gesturing as if lost. I smiled. Tried to look friendly. See the stupid American? Just took a wrong turn, that's all, buddy. Just lead me toward the bar and we'll both be happy.

But it didn't work. I heard the metallic *click* as he flicked off the safety of the automatic, and he came at me in a weighty jog.

My mind scanned frantically, searching for some way to take him. If I had a knife, I could try a quick throw, then roll for my life, hoping for a lucky hit. But the stout Gerber was folded away in its belt holder, and even if I made a try for it the 7.62mm slugs would cut me in two like something meant for the toaster.

Face it, MacMorgan. Your luck's run out. You knew the time would come; knew before the first mission that vultures don't give without finally taking. And you always lied to yourself, told yourself that you'd accept it willingly—told yourself that you had loved well and lived fully, and had killed vultures enough to warrant the price of your own frail heartbeat. So why the sweaty palms, the hot weight upon your chest? Because you will never be ready. No one ever is. . . .

But my luck hadn't run out.

I had the unexpected good fortune of falling in with a kindred spirit, a copper-haired, red-bearded, crazy-eyed Irishman by the name of Westy O'Davis.

And when the soldier went trotting by the narrow intersection of corridors, O'Davis stepped out with a blind-sided overhand right that allowed the bulky Cuban one staggering step before he went down like a sack of wet bones.

O'Davis stepped out touching his knuckles gingerly. He looked at me and grinned. " 'Tis an interestin' life you live, brother MacMorgan."

I exhaled heavily. "Next time I tell you to stay out of my business, O'Davis, give me a swift kick in the ass, okay?"

"Pleasure, Yank. You're a man who needs watchin', I'm thinkin'."

Behind me, the muffled voice of Androsa's captors were louder now, closer to the door. I long-stepped it down the hall and helped the big Irishman drag the body of the soldier into the little storage room. I heard the cabin door open, and then voices. They were coming our way. The storage room was crammed with boxes, but we forced our way in, pulling the door halfway shut behind us. It smelled of mold and diesel, and overhead bare steampipes rattled and clanked with uneven pressure.

Waiting, I reached down and touched the soldier's neck. Fast-pulse. Steady.

"Dead?"

I shook my head. "No."

O'Davis looked surprised but said nothing.

We watched them go by: Androsa and two men. One wore the uniform of a common Cuban soldier. He had the woman's arm bent up behind her, and her mouth was a thin line of pain. Below the small head wound she had gotten back on *Storm Nest* was a larger swelling, fresh and already turning the soft cheek purple. The other Cuban was a hugely fat man, gaudy general's uniform draped over him like a tent. His face was a mass of rolling jowls and sweat, and his narrow pig eyes wavered only once: Androsa struggled as they passed before us, and he turned only just enough to slap her savagely across the face.

I felt the hand of Westy O'Davis holding my shoulder tightly, and heard him whisper in my ear, "Easy, mate. Easy . . ."

In the bright anger of that moment, detail stood out sharp and vivid, focusing through eyes and etched upon brain: tiny brave raven-haired woman locked between the bulk of the two soldiers. She wore an orange blouse. It brought out the deep tan and whitened the clenched teeth. Her blouse was ripped slightly at the collar, and two buttons were missing, knots of white thread twisted. She wore faded jeans and jogging shoes that squeaked against the linoleum as they forced her along, and the beautiful Spanish-Indian face masked its fear with a stoic hatred.

When their footsteps disappeared up the stairs, we shut the storage-room door behind us and stepped out into the corridor.

"This is where you get off, O'Davis. Things are gonna start to get real nasty from here on out."

He tugged at his red beard, keeping a close eye on the corridors as we walked along. "Like I said, Yank—you look like a man who needs lookin' after. Take the way you're walkin', fer instance. Too fast, mate—way too fast. Gotta walk outta here like we just bought this bloody ship."

I looked at him, suspicious. "You sound like you've done this sort of thing before."

He grinned, still casting glances before and behind us. "Ah! I have, I have—an' usually escapin' from an angry husband, I might add. But when I visit you in Key West I'll tell you all about *that.* Now it's the lass we're after—and a fine-lookin' woman, too."

"So you're the one who understands Spanish. Tell me what they were saying."

"Your lady wasn't sayin' much. Swearin' some—an' a talented job of it, too. The fat chap—hoggish fella, weren't he?—he mentioned Pier Two. Expect they're headed that way."

"Anything else?"

He thought for a moment. "Aye. There is. Got the name of the fat fellow. Soldier used it once. Damn general he is—guess you'd have to be a general to be that fat in a country as poor as this. Strange name, like a bird. Called him General Halcón. Means 'Hawk' in Spanish. . . ."

15

They left in one of the small twin-engine patrol skiffs. It was about twenty-one feet long, made of wood and painted gray, with enough muscle in the inboard-outboards to blast it across the calm harbor like a shaft of pale light. Top speed probably sixty to sixty-five mph. It was patrol boat number 13—one of only two I had seen loaded with soldiers flying around Mariel. In a craft that fast, there was no way we could keep an eye on them. So I had to take O'Davis's word that they were headed for Pier Two.

The two of us went lumbering back through the bar, and outside, our faces were masks of relaxed confidence. Soldiers rushed past us without hesitating. A couple of second-place finishers in the fight lay on the deck groaning. As O'Davis said, confident people don't draw attention. And he was right about our taxi driver, too—he still sat in the skiff waiting for us, patient as an old horse.

It was sunset. A scarlet dusk with the sun's rays lancing through the acid factory smog. The rays were set apart in shafts of ruddy light, hitting boats and crimson clouds and the castle hulk of the stone Naval Academy like stage lights.

In his guttural Spanish, O'Davis whipped our driver into reluctant action. He steered us through the maze of shrimp boats, cruisers, and ratty commercial trawlers at a stately twenty knots, the displacement wake leaving the waiting boats rolling behind us. There was nothing I could do but think and wait. Westy tugged at his red beard and hummed some Gaelic tune, *tum-de-dum dum dum,* while I tried to formulate a plan. Once we got to Pier Two, there wasn't much I could do. Or needed to do. I had to find out where they were keeping the woman. It would be better if they had stuck her on a bus and taken her into Havana, the Triton Hotel maybe. I knew my way around Havana—it couldn't be changed that much even in twenty years. And once I knew where she was, I could plan my rescue. I had the explosives aboard *Sniper.* A charge here, a charge there. Get the Castro Cubans confused, get them running. And there was always my crossbow. Silent and deadly. I felt the old coldness move through me, felt the assiduous warrior-man that I had once been—and would always be—take control of my mind. All I needed was data. There would be no indecision now. Reanchor at the most secluded spot in the harbor I could find, and then . . .

I felt the Irishman staring at me. There was a studious look of reevaluation on his face; he looked like a kid who just discovered the garter snake in his hands was really a cottonmouth. He said, "I doon't know what's on yer mind, Yank—but whatever it is, I'm glad I'm ta be on your side. Them sea-colored eyes of yours are a wee bit too revealin'. Do me a favor now, an' doon't let the soldiers catch you lookin' like you jest were. They'll throw us both in the cooler without a fare-thee-well."

I slapped him on the shoulder. "You're right, O'Davis. I was just thinking about the way . . . the way they were treating that woman."

"Aye, I know what ya mean. It brings out the blackness in us, mate. Strange, in a way. You come ta hate somethin' so much that, in time, you become the thing you hate. A dictatorship is a government of the frightened and the savage. An' from the looks of ya, Yank, you aren't a man to become frightened. Now look over there, will ya?"

He pointed to an expanse of concrete wharf where there were cement-block buildings. Boats crowded around the wharf, and there were big fuel-tank cylinders by a wooden machine shop at the end of a short canal. But mostly there were people: three long lines of weary-looking men, women, and children, heads down, shuffling and somber in the growing darkness. The wharf was heavily guarded. A searchlight and a machine gun were mounted atop the highest building, and soldiers brushed by the line of refugees as if they did not exist.

O'Davis made a sweeping gesture with his big

hands. "That's what this is all about, Yank. That's Pier Three—where they herd the refugees onto boats. Now look at them poor folk there, will ya? They're the frightened in the camp of the savages. An' the head savage is round here someplace—that ya kin bet on."

I was surprised. "Castro?"

He shrugged. "He's a bit of a dark prince, ya know. Imagine this is the sort a thing 'e wouldn't miss seein'. Got no permanent presidential palace or anything like that—not his style. Besides, he's gotta keep movin' or his own people would lay in wait for him, an' assassinate him, I expect. What I'm sayin', Yank, is we gotta be very careful. With the big man around, the soldiers are not goin' to take any chances of lettin' things get outta hand—if ya see what I mean."

"I see," I said. "And that's exactly why you're going back to that pretty schooner of yours once you introduce me to Pier Two."

"Oh, I will, I will. After I've had me a beer or two. I'm not goin' to let a big ugly brute like yerself get me inta trouble. Are ya thinkin' me a fool?"

I sneered at his sly grin. "I suppose you're going to promise me again, huh?"

"Ah do, ah do—on the grave of me very own mother."

Pier Two was a dirt strip sided by canvas booths where bored Cuban vendors sold beer and cigars, T-shirts, fighting cocks, beans and yellow rice, and moldy slabs of bacon shiny with flies. A string of bare two-hundred-watt bulbs threw a carnival glare on the Cuban-Americans who stood on the dirt road drinking beer and shielding themselves from the guards with a careful hilarity. It was north of Pier Three by about a half mile, located between the water and the belching stacks of the power plant, and chain-link fence topped by barbed wire enclosed the area. Our driver nosed up to the makeshift plywood dock, cracked his propeller on the rocks which surrounded the dock, and we left him cursing the skiff with subdued emotion.

"Well, well, well," O'Davis said, his sarcasm taking grand form. "I wonder what the poor folks back in the U.S.A. are doin' tonight, Yank."

"Pretty place, no doubt about that," I said. "Appropriately decorated, too."

The big Irishman saw what I was pointing at—a swollen rat, oil-covered, lifting and falling in the water wash around the docks.

"Ah, the poor little bugger. Ate some of th' food here, no doubt."

I followed O'Davis through the crowd of people. He was obviously no stranger to the place. Cuban-American men singled him out, greeting him heartily in enthusiastic Spanish. While he stopped to talk with a couple of them, I worked my way up to the plank bar.

"*Dos cervezas, por favor.*"

The skinny vendor squinted at me, turned without a word, and took two Hatuey beers from the trough of ice behind him. I handed him a five, and he handed me back a one.

"Hold it there, Yank!" O'Davis came ambling up beside me. "The little snit short-changed ye."

He wheeled on the Cuban, barked an abrupt command. The vendor glared at him momentarily, then laid two more ones on the counter.

"O'Davis," I said, "I'm trying to figure out what goodness I've done in my life for God to send me my very own guardian angel."

"Hah! Hardly an angel, Yank. Hardly that. Ye've been around some, I kin see that, mate. That scar on yer face didna come from disco dancin', I'm thinkin'. An' you've used them knuckles o' yers for more than itchin' yer own nose. But you've never been to a place as nasty as Mariel Harbor, Yank." He looked at me for a moment, then smiled. "But then again, maybe ya have."

"Maybe," I said. "Even so, I was damn lucky to run into someone as foolish as you."

He raised his eyebrows in mock offense. "Foolish, am I? Well, let me tell you, Mr. Dusky MacMorgan American citizen, I'm the fool what jest got some very important information fer ya."

"And that is?"

He took me by the arm and pulled me away from the crowded outdoor bar. Down the dirt road, people ate beans and rice from cardboard containers. Guards stood at the one-lane exit gate, and men crowded around a crate while a Cuban vendor washed down a wild-eyed fighting cock with Aguadiente, a cheap fusel rum. We made seats out of beer crates in the shadows.

"The information is this, Yank. Forty-five minutes ago was the last time one of their bloody buses left for Havana. An' the next one isn't due for fifteen minutes. One of me chums told me."

"So the woman's still around here someplace."

"Unless they carted her off in a government jeep— or never brought her here in the first place."

"I hope you didn't ask your friends if they saw the woman, because you never know—"

"I'll not even dignify that question with an answer, if ye don't mind."

"Sorry." I thought for a moment. If she was still in the area, where would they be keeping her? There were a couple of wooden, tin-roofed buildings by the exit gate: some kind of guard quarters, probably. There was a light on in the smallest of the two, and an armed soldier stood outside. O'Davis seemed to read my mind.

"Could be, Yank. Might be keepin' her there till the next bus comes along. Or they might jest take her down the road a piece to Pier Three." He hesitated, then asked, "Ya know, Dusky, I might be able ta help ye more if ya told me why they took her. What is she, some kinda bloody spy or somethin'?"

I kept my face blank. "Guess you're right, Westy. Fact is, I'm not really sure why they took her. Something to do with her American citizenship papers not being in order or something."

He chuckled softly and said nothing.

"And what's that supposed to mean?" I said.

"Yank, it's a bad liar ye are. Too much Scotch blood in ye an' not enough Irish, I'm thinkin'. No, don't argue with me. I'll not ask ya any more questions."

"Good. I'm going to hold you to that. And I'm also going to hold you to your promise to get the hell out of here once I know my way around. I know my way around, O'Davis. And it's time for you to leave."

"So you kin do what?" He said it too loud, and he immediately lowered his voice. He crouched over, sticking his red face in mine. "So you kin stroll up ta that wee bit of shack, knock on the door, an' tell 'em to turn your woman loose? They'll shoot ya down, Yank. I've seen two men killed in this blasted harbor already, an' I'll not let me new mate play the fool for the likes o' them!"

"O'Davis, you're big and tough and bullheaded, no doubt about that. But goddammit, believe me when I say that you're going to be in over that Irish head of yours if you don't start listening. You're out of your league, O'Davis. Now, dammit, get the hell out of here before I show you just how tough you really are!"

Offended, he took on an air of burlesque aloofness. "Out of me league, am I? Well, tell me, Yank—jest what *do* you plan to do?"

"I plan to sit right here, wait on the next bus, and see just who gets on it."

"An' if she's not among 'em, then what?"

I shook my head wearily. "O'Davis, were you born stubborn, or do you have to work at it? If the woman doesn't get on that bus, then I'm going to find out where she is, snake her away from the Cubans, then head my boat for American water just as fast as I can. It's going to be messy, you Irish fool, and some people are going to end up pretty damn dead—and I don't want you to be one of them! There, have I made myself understood?"

"Ah, ye have, ye have." He stood up as if to leave.

"But I appreciate your help," I said quickly. "And the invitation to visit me in Key West still stands." I stuck out my hand as a final sign of friendship.

He looked at me, looked at the outstretched hand, confusion in his face. "Why, ya doon't think . . . I'm not leavin' for *good*, Yank. Jest stood up to stretch me legs and get us a coupla more beers." He stuck out his palm, as if testing for rain. "Sure, 'twas an interestin' little speech ye give me. But it's a fine soft night and, if you doon't mind, I'll stick around for a while longer and join ye in conversation while ye wait."

He moved as if to go to the bar, then turned back to me. "I've taken a likin' to ya, brother MacMorgan. After twenty-two days o' sittin' round this hellish harbor, I'm not about ta miss me one chance for a little excitement. Besides, I've luck enough for six men, an' I'm a-thinkin' yer goin' to need all the luck you kin get. . . ."

*   *   *

I didn't even see them coming. I was doing one of my little stunts. Cute little stunt, MacMorgan. Let your concentration sag for a moment, and watch your new friend die. . . .

The bus for Havana came and left. Big Spanish-made bus, all chrome and steel, looking totally out of place alongside the wooden-wheeled cart that followed it in, bored donkey and bored driver *clip-cloppa-clipping* along the dirt road, hauling a fresh load of beer for the *tiendas.* The donkey was gray with a white blaze on chest and forehead. Sweat lathered around its harness, and it wore a straw cane cutter's hat, holes for pointed ears, implying some affection on the part of the somnolent old man who was driving. The donkey pulled to a rolling stop in front of the beer trough without a word from its owner.

Sitting on my crate seat, I watched the bus make its hydraulic *pee-e-esh* as doors opened and Cuban-Americans began to unload after their trip to the Triton Hotel in Havana. A guard stood at the door of the bus checking their packages as they exited. The Cuban-Americans accepted the indignity of being searched with a remote indifference that sent a strange surge of pride through me. Here they were in their native land, seeking only to help their loved ones, and yet the Castro regime was treating them like criminals. But they were Americans, an immigrant people who had fought before for their self-respect, and they weren't about to give the guard the satisfaction of reacting to his slights. One by one they filed off, somber-faced, but filled with the strength of their own dignity.

Once the bus was empty, the driver came off, lit a cigarette, and sat on the bottom step while a ludicrous pipe-organ version of "On Top of Old Smoky" came tinnily through the speakers of the bus.

People began to line up outside the door of the bus, waiting patiently to pay their fifteen dollars for the return trip to Havana.

I felt my shallow breaths and my heart pounded heavily in my ears as I waited for the door of the little guard shack to open. A light was on inside, and a silhouette moved before the window: a hugely fat man, cheeks hanging as slack as empty balloons.

No doubt about the man's identity: one general Halcón, code name Hawk.

For once in your life, Stormin' Norman Fizer, you lied to me. You told me Halcón was one of the good guys. You told me he had defected, pledged his new allegiance to America and to the destruction of the Castro regime. But he's the one who took my new love; the one who slapped her across the face as if she were some disobedient dog. You were wrong, Stormin' Norman. Wrong, wrong, wrong, and only Halcón's corpse will atone for the lie. . . .

The driver threw his cigarette onto the ground without snuffing it and called for the people to board. "On Top of Old Smoky" had changed to pipe-organ calypso. The new group filed on, heads held high, and I waited for the guard-shack door to open; waited for them to shove Androsa out and onto the bus so I could follow along and, with luck, mark the room at the Triton Hotel which would become her final prison.

But the door never opened. Halcón's mass passed once more before the window, then was gone. The doors of the bus *pee-e-eshed* closed, and then it powered back through the exit gates in a cloud of dust and invisible diesel exhaust.

"So it's not ta Havana they're takin' her, eh, Yank?"

O'Davis stood before me, two beers in hand, watching the bus disappear.

"Nothing to do but wait," I said.

He read the quality in my voice. "Cheer up, brother MacMorgan. Cheer up, lad. All across America there are folks a-rottin' their brains before the television tubes on this fine night, waitin' ta die, while we're down here, fine men with the courage of a plan, jest waitin' to take life by the throat."

I looked at him and couldn't help but smile. "Do you realize, O'Davis, that you are eye deep in bull-shit?"

"Not only realize it, Yank—but am very proud to admit it meself. Ah am, ah am."

So we drank the cold beer, talked and waited.

Westy O'Davis was not only an entertaining talker, he was a fine listener as well; one of those rare people you meet and immediately feel as if you have known a lifetime. He was one of those unusual people who follows conversation down branches, exploring veins of thought with the delight of a discoverer, mixing little truths with dark Irish humor. He told me how he had followed Castro's takeover of Cuba, fascinated with a man so dedicated to a cause that he would spend his youth hiding out in mainland mountains and on offshore islands just waiting until the time was ripe for revolution.

"True, I admired him fer a time—jest as them newspaper an' broadcast folk in yer own country are still naive enough ta admire him. But then I came to realize he was jest one more dictator insane with the want of power, as brutal as he was charmin'. And for the likes o' us ta fight it, Yank, will do no more good than pissin' inta a stout wind." He laughed and slapped his leg. "But ain't that what men like you and meself are built fer? A life battlin' the evil wind. An' what more could a real man want, Yank?"

They came for us when he was on his second trip to the canvas *tienda:* a copper-haired, red-bearded sea rover but always the dark son of Ireland, ambling broad shoulder, hands in pockets, head bowed slightly, wanting more beer because it was a fine soft night with a hint of wind.

I hadn't noticed them pulling up in the twin-engine patrol boat: Captain Lobo, feral-faced Zapata, three heavily armed sailors in baggy blue uniforms, and the soldier O'Davis had cold-cocked, back on the *Pinares,* bandage around his head.

O'Davis saw them before I did. I watched in vague surprise as the soldier with the bandage scanned the crowd at Pier Two, then locked in on me. He pointed, dark eyes fierce.

He yelled something in Spanish. Lobo nodded as if not surprised, then barked orders to his complement of assassins. They came at me, violence on their faces, AK-47 assault rifles beaded on my head.

And that's when O'Davis made his move. He stumbled out into the three of them as if hopelessly drunk, secure for a time in the knowledge that the soldier with the bandage had never seen the man who had hit him. They shoved him roughly away, but back he came, playing the role of the sloppy drunk, trying to give me time to run, to escape, to get the hell away from Pier Two and Mariel Harbor before it was too late. And then one of the sailors cracked him in the face with the butt of his rifle, a glancing blow to the chin. And the Irishman went down hard on his rump. I saw his face blanch and the blue eyes narrow, and for an instant it was like looking in some long-gone reflection of my own face.

Westy O'Davis was not a man to be sent to the ground without a fight—a fight to the death.

The soldiers were maybe twenty-five yards from me when the Irishman got back on his feet. They were concentrating on me, not the drunk they had left bleeding behind. He hit the guard who had clubbed him at full stride, head down, shoulder bulling into the sailor's spine like an NFL linebacker hellbent on destruction. The sailor's neck jerked back with a loud *ker-RACK* like a tree limb bursting, and O'Davis came up rolling, AK-47 in his hands. In two explosive bursts, he cut the other two sailors into wilting heaps.

I was on my feet now. The soldiers from the guard-house were running, vectoring in on the Irishman, opening fire. I hit the first one thigh-high, feeling his knee crumple beneath the impact. But he refused to give up the rifle. I wrestled with him desperately, watching in the slow-motion horror of the moment as the Irishman died.

Zapata, a rattish leer on his face, had an automatic weapon in his thin hands. He didn't know how to use the rifle. It swung wildly in his arms, throwing flames. The old man stood by the cart holding the reins of the sleepy donkey with the straw hat. As the old man watched, shocked, his face suddenly splin-tered and disappeared into a sludge of crimson. The donkey went down braying, bullet-sprayed, legs kicking like a dreaming dog on the run. O'Davis didn't have a chance. He had made the good fight; battled the evil wind to the end. And as I watched Zapata level the AK-47 at him, I knew that it was over for the two of us; knew that the vultures had finally taken their pound of flesh, and then there was a bright light erupting in my brain and then there was darkness. . . .

16

I awoke to a dull cranial ache as if my brain had been vinylized and stuffed with cotton. Bright corona around the white light over my face. Numbness of face and hands.

A voice: "Can you hear me, Capitán MacMorgan?"

Heavy Spanish accent. Voice I remembered . . . from where?

I sat bolt upright, head swiveling. I wasn't dead, and I wasn't in a prison. Surprised, I put odors of bottom paint, diesel, and familiar surrounds together: I was back aboard *Sniper*.

Captain Lobo, his heavy face perspiring, stood over me. He said, "So you are awake, Capitán MacMorgan. Good."

He seemed somehow relieved.

I got shakily to a sitting position, wiping face with hands. I expected to see blood, but there was none. Lobo stood at the entranceway of *Sniper*'s master berth. Behind him were three soldiers, cramping the narrow quarters of my boat, filling it with an odor of tobacco smoke and sweat.

"Where's O'Davis?" I tried to stand, but Lobo pushed me back.

"Dead, I assume." No trace of emotion when he said it. He paused for a moment, looking at me. And then: "You and your friend put us in a very awkward position, MacMorgan. If I had my way, gringo, you would have been dead an hour ago. But . . . I have my orders." He turned and said something to the soldiers. Obediently, they left the cabin, closing the door behind them. He paused, took out a cigarette, and lit it with great deliberation. "Before one of my men clubbed you," he said, "three Americans—Cuban-Americans—were killed in the firing your friend so stupidly caused."

"He didn't—"

"No, your friend did not kill them," Lobo interrupted. "Unfortunately, one of our officers did—but it doesn't matter who killed them. They're dead. As you know, my country holds your country in something less than contempt. Capitalism—hah! The rich get richer, no?"

"I'll pass on the political lectures, if you don't mind, Lobo."

The smile he always wore became evident, edged with a sneer.

"As I was about to say, *Capitán*: My country holds yours in contempt, but it is still a force to be reckoned with. And the fact that three Americans have been shot to death here . . . well, the possible political repercussions are obvious. Because of that, at this moment, Radio Havana is preparing to broadcast a statement blaming the killings on a few poorly organized anti-Castro Cubans—revolutionaries who attacked and killed randomly until our forces were able to turn them back. Of course, you and the other Americans who witnessed what happened will claim otherwise. But it will be just your word against ours—"

"And you can hardly get away with killing everyone who was there, right?" I finished.

"Exactly." It was a hard, thin smile now. He reached into his shirt pocket and extracted a sheet of paper. He unfolded it and glanced over it briefly.

"Capitán MacMorgan, how well did you know the woman you brought to Mariel—Androsa Santarun?"

I tried to keep my face empty and my voice neutral. "Not too well, really. Her lawyer contacted me. Paid me fifteen thousand dollars to bring her over here so she could try to take her father back to America." I tried an extra bit of truth to keep the story believable. "I, ah . . . we became lovers while we were here."

He didn't take his eyes from the paper. "Then that explains it, *Capitán.*"

"Explains what?"

"Why she insisted that you not be killed." He lifted his dark dead eyes from the paper for the first time. "Capitán MacMorgan, Androsa Santarun is a spy. Please, no look of surprise. It makes no differ-

ence if you knew it or not. As far as we know, she
has no family living in Cuba. There was a half
brother"—he shrugged—"but he is dead. Señorita
Santarun is the fourth American spy to come to Mariel Harbor. The first three came foolishly believing
they could find and then assassinate Presidente Fidel
Castrol. Luckily, the same agent who informed us of
their intentions also assured us that they were rene-
gades, and not sent by your country—"

"You mean you people have agents in
Washington—"

He silenced me with a threatening look. "You are
not here to ask questions, *Capitán*. You are alive only
so that you can listen and carry a message back to
your people. I was about to tell you that those three
agents are dead—all killed, unfortunately, before
they could be . . . *interrogar* . . . interrogated."

"So now you plan to force the woman to talk."

"There is hardly need to *force* her, *Capitán*." He
made a face as if offended at being so misunderstood.
"Señorita Santarun has, of her own free will, defected." He handed me the paper he had been holding, ignoring the look of shock that I felt slip across
my face. "If she could have been forced into telling
us the secrets of your government, would we even
bother with a formal paper of defection from her?
No, certainly not. As you can see, the letter is signed
in her own hand—and of her own free will. But as
you probably know, Capitán MacMorgan, she is a
stubborn woman, and she will not begin to truly co-
operate with us until you are safely back in the

United States." He checked his watch. "Soon, our patrol boats will escort you out of Mariel Harbor. Once you reach Key West, you are to radio a message on VHF 11. You are to give the name of a book you gave your lover, Señorita Santarun. There is no way we could know what book that might be, and so the correct title will be proof to the señorita that she is not being tricked. You will send the message once every fifteen minutes over the period of an hour to make sure we receive it clearly." Captain Lobo checked his watch again. "I suggest you hurry, Capitán MacMorgan. If you are not back in Key West in . . . twenty-four hours? . . . then we must assume something has happened to you. And that will make the señorita useless to us, so we will kill her. Until then, she rests at a very pleasant cottage at the Naval Academy, awaiting *your* cooperation."

He turned and left without another word.

So do your job, MacMorgan. The woman was the bait and the tiger finally got her, so hustle on back to that gaudy little pirate town at the end of A1A and report to Norm Fizer. It's what everyone wants you to do—from Castro's gun-loving puppets to your own dear government. Sure, Androsa Santarun was something special, but so what? And Westy O'Davis was one of those rare guys you want to count as a friend for a lifetime, but they had shot him dead and there's nothing you can do. So carry out your orders, MacMorgan, because that's what you're supposed to do, and you're a man who has always and forever followed orders . . . right?

Wrong. . . .

*   *   *

Somewhere in the Havana night would be a radar antenna whirling attentively, tracking me on a thirty-to-forty-mile scan. Not all that tough to beat it, really. The drug runners have it down to a science. And once upon a time I had studied the methods and ploys of drug runners in the same way an osprey studies the convolutions of schooling mullet.

One of the antiquated gunboats led me out of the harbor. It was three a.m. by the green glow of my Rolex watch. I steered from the main controls, head aching slightly, red chart light letting my eyes stroll across the map of mainland Cuba, memorizing exactly what I must do. For the hell of it, I took the overhead mike in hand and tried to raise the Key West marine operator. It wouldn't hurt to try to get a double-edged message to Norm Fizer. But the Cubans jammed me, as I knew they would.

Four miles out to sea, the lights of Havana began to fall away, lifting, holding, and finally sinking in my wake. Starry night, two days past the quarter moon. Florida Straits were still busy with frail red and green glow of distant running lights. The Freedom Flotilla was still going full tilt, hell-bent on carrying as many refugees to the freedom dream of America before the two big C's—Castro and Carter—got together and decided too many people were dying in that torturous expanse of water and, besides, neither of them was benefiting from it as they thought they would.

Plenty of American boats still making the crossing

to Mariel Harbor. And that was good. I needed the boats for cover.

About twenty miles out, close to international waters, the gunboat suddenly backed engines and turned around. For one wild second, I thought they had stopped to sweep their guns across *Sniper;* stopped to send me to the bottom right there without a trace. But they hesitated only long enough to pick up a course back to Mariel Harbor, then rumbled away into the black wash of night sea. I didn't wait around to watch. I shoved both throttles ahead full bore, feeling the burst of acceleration pull my head back. The Si-Tex radar screen, bolted above the cabin controls, was throwing small bursts of green light across the grid, and I headed for the biggest pack of boats I could find at a crashing thirty-four knots.

I ran an unyielding rum line for almost twenty minutes before I picked up the first white mastlights of the small flotilla bound for Mariel, starlike on the horizon. I grabbed the Bushnell zoom scope and got a rolling look at them: three cruisers and a ragged trawler. I switched off my running lights and swept out around them, keeping my distance. And when I had a clean angle, I flipped the running lights back on and approached from their stern. I was probably well out of Havana radar range. But even if I wasn't, it wouldn't matter. On a grid big enough to scan forty miles, they would lose me among the indistinct blur of the other boats.

So I pulled throttles back and stayed tight astern of the four other boats. They were making about

fourteen knots, and when I had my speed adjusted
to theirs, I locked the Benmar autopilot in temporarily while I got a cold Hatuey beer from the cooler
and added a healthy pinch of Copenhagen between
lip and gum. I felt the old anticipation come over
me; the good feeling of the hunter on the track of
the deserving prey. In about fourteen hours, the Castro gun goons were going to get the surprise of their
lives. Their job was to stop unauthorized Cubans
from getting out of Mariel—and they wouldn't be
expecting a blind-sided attack from someone trying
to get *in*. Still, I had to have some luck. The narrow
untended tidal creek the chart showed to be west of
Mariel Harbor would have to be deep enough for me
to get in. And there would have to be cover enough
for me to camouflage *Sniper*. And, also, the Cubans
would have to fall for the drug runners' radio-
distress ploy that would explain my final disappearance. But I had already had the best kind of luck.
Radio Havana had, according to Lobo, reported an
attack on Mariel by a band of anti-Castro Cubans.
They would have no choice but to explain the second
attack in the same way. . . .

The tidal river was deep enough. But not by much.
I had pulled away from my screen of boats an hour
before sunrise three miles offshore. It's not true about
it being always darkest before the dawn. Not on the
open ocean, anyway. There was no sun, but the sea
took on a pearly luminescence. The water changed
from black to turquoise—a turquoise of such inten-

sity that it seemed as if it would discolor the black hull of my cruiser. The wind freshened, blowing waves across the bow. And the rolling expanse of sea, wind, and waves seemed energized by an incandescence of its own, as if the radiance had been accumulated over a million days beneath the Gulf Stream sun.

Below Mariel Harbor, it was a wilderness coast: cliffs topped by banyan trees and yellow bamboo. A rivulet toppled down one hillside, ending in a waterfall that sprayed down onto the rocks and sea below. Wind brought the scent of the mainland over the water, and it smelled of dank earth and frangipani and jasmine. The river I was seeking would be somewhere dead ahead, beyond the reef, and it was time for me to make my disappearance official. To the people in the radar room, I would be some unknown vessel hopelessly off course, searching for Mariel. Now the unknown vessel would sink.

I took the mike in my hand and, ridiculously, tried to disguise my voice—as if anyone in Cuba would know my voice:

Mayday, mayday, this is the power vessel Assail . . . *we've hit some coral . . . boat's going down fast . . . engine's on fire . . . need assistance immediately. . . .*

I repeated the message three times, adding bogus loran coordinates—four miles from my true position— to the name of the imaginary vessel. After the last transmission, my voice straining with a quality of panic, I mimicked a loud *woofing* explosion, then let the set go dead.

Good luck, Cubans. You rarely answer an American distress call anyway—no matter where it's at. But if you do come in search of the damaged Assail *you'll find nothing. And that will make us both happy. . . .*

Quickly I hustled up to the flybridge. The reef lay ahead, and I wanted some visual altitude to run it. The sun was a fiery haze in the east now, and the coral stood out black below transparent waves and green sea. I powered along the seaward edge of it, looking for the current thrust from the river which I knew would create a natural channel through the reef.

And there it was: a snaking path of olive water through the coralheads and staghorn which led to calm water beyond the reef, and then a narrow entranceway of water guarded by mainland buttonwood and black mangrove trees—the tidal river.

I considered not marking the channel with the plastic milk bottles weighted with lead I had made— but then decided I had to take the risk of their being noticed. I would be leaving by darkness, probably, and ramming *Sniper* up onto the reef would leave me stranded in Cuba.

And I couldn't afford to be stranded.

Not after what I had planned.

So I dropped three markers: one at the seaward exit, one at the narrowest bight, and the last at the river entrance to the reef. And then I nosed *Sniper* up the river at dead slow, sticking to the concave banks where the current would have dug out the deepest channel. It was one of those mangrove rivers with a vegetable bottom of muck and leaves. Heat came off the water, and limbs from mangroves slid across the hull of *Sniper* as we made our way. There was a dank and eerie silence about the narrow river interrupted only by the whine of mosquitoes and the occasional chatter of a kingfisher, and when my props kicked up mud, a visceral odor of sludge erupted behind.

The river deepened, narrowed even more, then branched into a crooked Y. I nosed up one branch, touched engines into reverse, then backed two boat lengths down the narrowest creek and switched off the engines.

I had a lot of work to do. I cut mangroves and covered those parts of *Sniper* which might be seen from the air, then went below and got the fake battery from the forward bilge.

"Until then, she's resting in a pleasant cottage at the Naval Academy," Lobo had told me.

The Naval Academy—the stone castle on the cliff above Mariel Harbor. Big mistake, Lobo. You should have never mentioned it.

I uncapped the battery and, once again, inventoried its deadly contents.

Plenty enough to do the job.

I was sweating from my work with the machete cutting tree limbs, so I grabbed a towel and wiped at my face while I went through my drawers beneath the master berth, looking for pencil and paper. I knew what I wanted to do: jerk everything I could remember about the terrain around the Naval Academy to the mental surface, then make a detailed map. Circles would represent guard outposts. X's would mark where I would put the explosives. I wanted to work out every possible means of escape, including the possible use of another tidal creek that branched off a finger of Mariel Harbor and, according to the chart, dead-ended only a mile or two from the mangrove river where I now waited. Repetition and concentration—I wanted to sear every alternative into my mind so completely that I wouldn't have to take time to think. Because, in the circumstances of war, makeshift planning can leave you very dead indeed.

So it was while rummaging through the drawers looking for paper and pen that I found it.

The book I had given Androsa Santarun to read: H. M. Tomlinson's *The Sea and the Jungle.* It was placed on top of a pile of miscellaneous gear, face down, spine crinkled, opened to her place. The instant irritation I felt at seeing so rare a book treated so badly was replaced by the immediate realization that I had returned the book once to the ammo-box library.

But was it before Androsa left *Sniper* or after?

I couldn't remember.

I picked it up carefully, closed it. But there was something wrong. The book closed—but not properly; just the slightest spring of foreign matter between pages. I leafed through the fine old volume and found it: a letter to me from Androsa. I remembered her that day atop the flybridge writing and reading, using my stomach as a pillow. So she had been writing to me—and had used the strange code message I was to send from Key West to tell me where to look.

I took out the letter, unfolded it, and read it quickly. Then I dropped the note on the bunk, went to the icebox, and got a beer, because I needed it. And then I read the letter again, still in shocked disbelief.

My Dearest Dusky—

I write this now because I know they will be calling for me soon and that I will leave you and never see you again. In a way, leaving you will be the hardest thing, but it is something I must do. The last two years of my life have been very dark years, Dusky. And for a short time you brought some light to them. I can't allow myself to think how it might be if we could be together longer, because it is impossible, and there is nothing sadder than hoping for the impossible. You think you know about me, Dusky, but you don't. But I know about you. This morning while you made breakfast I found a piece of torn paper. It was just a corner you had overlooked, but it was enough to tell me it was a CIA bio sheet, and I know now what I had suspected—that you are more than a charterboat captain. For some reason, I was disappointed to find it. But I know that you were sent to help in some way, but you cannot help.

I mentioned that I had a half brother who was killed by Castro's men. That is true, Dusky, but I did not know until we found that sinking boat, *Storm Nest*. The man who had been murdered so horribly was my own dear, dear Alvino. His father, who is a good man, married my mother and adopted me. I loved my brother very much, so you can imagine what a horrible decision it was for me when, two years ago, a General Halcón approached me upon Castro's arrival in New York and, in secrecy, told me that if I did not help him pose as a double agent my brother would be killed. So for these last twenty-four months I have been, in truth, a double agent working against America, the country I love. I do not know how Alvino got the boat and tried to make his escape, but I do know it was the Cubans who trailed him and murdered him. The agent who died in my arms told me. Before his escape, Alvino had warned them of Halcón, and the agent had found out about my arrival and was coming to warn me when they killed him. That is when I realized just what a foul creature I have become, Dusky, because it was I who told the Cubans of the plot to kill Castro. I sentenced those three men to death, and now that my dear brother is gone I can atone for it. Or at least try to. You must not worry about me, Dusky. It is almost funny—the thing I hate so much will not allow them to kill me. . . ."

And then followed the number of a post office box which I was to give to my superior; the box contained, Androsa wrote, a list of secret information she had given the Cubans.

Sweat rolled down my nose and plopped onto the paper. I got another beer and sat down at the little galley booth. Mosquitoes had found my hiding place in the mangroves, and I swatted at them absently while rereading the letter, letting the woman I had loved and lost shed light on the past mysteries of Mariel.

But I hadn't truly lost her. Not yet. I finished puzzling over the strange wording of the letter's last sentence, then hid it away and turned my attention to drawing a good map of the terrain around the Naval Academy. I had already lost one of the rare people to "the stout wind." I wasn't about to lose another one.

17

So don the armor, MacMorgan. In days of yore it would be breastplate and plumed helmet and a two-handed sword forged from Spanish steel. Those were the days for you and the dead Irishman, MacMorgan; times when a man could set out on a good horse to right wrongs, slay the dragon, and do honorable battle with windmills and adversaries alike.

But now the armor is nothing more than the well-loved black Navy watch sweater, the lucky British commando knickers, and the face shadow from the olive-drab Special Forces tube. The sword is the waterproof knapsack on your back with its deadly cargo of RDX explosives and plenty of extra shafts for the Cobra crossbow slung over your shoulder. And the white steed is nothing more than your own good legs or, in a pinch, the Dacor TX-1000 competition fins you carry just in case. . . .

Strange thoughts as I moved through the black

marsh below the cane fields and the small village at the southern point of Mariel Harbor. Flashbacks and the haunting rush of *déjà vu: You have been here before, MacMorgan, for now and all time because this is what you do best and, deep in your brain, love most—the stalking of an enemy, like all warriors before and those to come. . . .*

I forced my mind clear. I was getting sloppy, letting my thoughts rove. I had been lucky so far. Everything had gone smoothly. Almost frighteningly smoothly.

I had worked my way cross-country from the tidal creek where *Sniper* was hidden to the backside of the peninsula with the little military outpost and amphibious landing strip and air tower. From a clump of bushes I had watched the soldiers walk the beach, ducking back into my cover with every sweep of the big searchlight. The beach was well fortified with bunkers and machine guns—but they didn't expect an attack from the mainland.

And so it was easy for me.

I had moved undetected through the rear of the encampment. Was close enough to one barracks to watch the off-duty soldiers laughing and smoking within the lighted window, planted quarter blocks of the RDX well behind the barracks, then added a half block at the foundation of the squat blue air tower. No mass slaughter, this—just enough explosives to bring the control tower toppling and to turn the night sky to bright day, but not close enough to do more than throw the soldiers unhurt from their bunks.

I had no desire—or reason—to kill hundreds. Just

wanted to get their attention so I could steal the lady back. But if someone got in my way . . .

So I had moved south through the night, down the west coast of the harbor. The American boats of the Freedom Flotilla rested at calm anchor, throwing white starpaths across the water with their cabin lights. Two thousand boats filled with desperate waiting people, ironically serene in the harbor—none of them knowing what was about to happen.

The marshland broke into firmer slough, and I made my way through the chest-high grass to the embankment where the dirt road began its twisting run up the cliff to the Naval Academy. I saw the flickering light of an approaching motorcycle and dove back into the grass until the rider was well out of sight.

The road would be the quickest route, but probably the most dangerous. So I hustled across the road and . . . and stopped dead in my tracks. I hadn't seen the soldier in the shadows by the tree. He was doing something. And then I realized: urinating. So I was right—the road was guarded. I dropped down onto my belly, feeling warm ditchwater seep through the wool watch sweater. He zipped up his pants, turned toward me. And just as I was about to rush him, cold steel of Randall attack-survival knife a good weight in right hand, the guard suddenly yelled and jumped back. I ducked at the first explosion of his automatic rifle, knowing that I had been seen and that I was a dead man. But the fire stopped abruptly. I watched the guard switch on a flashlight, reach down, and pick up a water moccasin as thick as my arm. Down the road, other guards were yelling, asking just what in the hell was going on. The soldier with the snake went lumbering down the road to show them.

I had no choice now. The dark thrust of wilderness before me was the only safe way to the stone castle atop the cliff. So climb it, MacMorgan. Hear the tranquil irony of owls calling and coons foraging through the brush while you pull yourself from tree to tree on a quarter-mile forty-degree grade and hope the woman is up there as she is supposed to be, and hope the dragon is somewhere nearby. . . .

Captain Lobo hadn't lied about the cottage. It was made of wood and roofed with tile, and it was very pleasant indeed. It was located in a clearing with other cottages—all billets, probably, for the Naval Academy students. But strangely, all the other cottages were empty, dark. It didn't make any sense. I rested in a clump of bamboo thinking. Too little sign of students, and a damn sight too many guards around the four-story stone block hulk of Academy. Maybe they had evacuated the students because of the influx of Americans to Mariel. But why?

Why . . .

Things had gone too smoothly. Emerson wrote about the one perfect law: compensation. Now the scale would swing back, because this part of my little journey would be deadly as hell. Twice I had almost been detected by guards on my approach to the string of cottages. One soldier had stood close enough for me to smell the sweat on his shirt. I could have killed either of them, but that would have ruined everything. I wasn't ready. Not yet.

I stayed in the shadows pulling myself along on my belly. Below, the searchlight from Pier Three scanned back and forth, painting the boats and the harbor in a stark white light. I took a final look through the window of the cottage and saw what I had hoped to see: Androsa Santarun, looking oddly more beautiful for her weariness, sitting in a straight-back chair leafing through a magazine. Captain Zapata sat across from her, AK-47 on his thin legs, watching her with a leer of unmistakable intent in his eyes. The massive bulk of General Halcón paced back and forth across the bare wooden floor, chain-smoking.

Hang on, good lady. It'll take me about twenty minutes to get everything set. And when I get back, Zapata and Halcón are going to get the Cobra crossbow cure for insomnia.

I worked my way to the drive which led down to the road. I RDX'ed the poles holding power terminals, located the three droplines which ran to telephones within the academy, and carefully cut one side of each line. If there was an incoming call, people inside could hear—but not be heard. And they could call out—but not be heard. Nothing suspicious about that. Phone trouble is the common complaint of the world. The main radio tower for the academy was down the road and up a bluff. I went unboth-

ered cross country and taped the final half block of
the explosive to that.

*Okay, Halcón, it's show time, you bastard. Your people
killed one very fine Irishman, and now you've stolen one
of the bravest and most beautiful women I have known.
It's show time, Halcón, and you're the main attraction.*

I waited a long time before crawling across the
clearing to the cottage again. One hundred yards
away, I could see the dim shapes of the guards moving about the perimeter of the stone academy. Small
orange eyes of their cigarettes glowed occasionally in
the darkness. A broad third-floor window was
lighted. Music filtered from it: the intricate inter-
sectings of a J.S. Bach fugue, the harpsicord music
seeming incongruous with the setting. A brown
shade was pulled the length of the window, and
against that scrim two men stood in silhouette.

And when I saw the silhouettes, I stopped.
Electrified.

*Jesus Christ, MacMorgan, you may have bought it this
time. Some great timing, buddy. Some perfect night to try
to bust up Mariel Harbor. . . .*

My breath coming harsh and shallow, I watched
the two men against the backlighted window. Even
at that distance their silhouettes were unmistakable.
One was the Hitchcock-like mass of General Halcón.
He had obviously left the cottage and gone into the
academy while I made my rounds. His head was
bowed slightly, jowls hanging. He said nothing, only
shrugged occasionally. The other man was doing all
the talking. He had a long ragged beard like some

dark prophet. Surprisingly, he did not wear the familiar field cap. But the long Cohiva cigar was there, and he used it to gesture as he spoke with great animation.

It was Fidel Castro.

As if in a trance, I felt my hands remove the sling of the Cobra crossbow. I mounted one of the aluminum shafts with the triangular killing point, then used the self-cocking slide to arm it. With deadly calm hands, I lined up the custom-built sights on the expanse of window, zeroing in on the dot between head and beard. If I pulled the trigger, the arrow would cover the hundred-yard distance in just under one second. It would burst through the glass like a .357 slug through tissue paper, and probably exit on the other side of Castro's temple.

But I didn't pull the trigger.

I couldn't. It was just the childish termination of the hunter sighting the forbidden game; the culmination of some macabre force within me that demanded all but the final step. And I thought:

If I were any one of two million Cuban-Americans—or any one of seventy percent of your own people—you would be dead right now. And if it weren't for ten thousand Americans sitting down there in that harbor you might be dead anyway.

A sound nearby made me lower the crossbow—a heavy rustle of bushes between me, and the window where the dictator still lectured Halcón. I watched the bushes tremble slightly, then stop. I waited, won-

dering if a guard and a machine gun might be positioned within the clump of foliage.

But then I could wait no more.

I had to move and move fast. I knew my plan was
sound. There would be no trouble killing the woman's guard—or guards—quickly and noiselessly. And
with the RDX planted at broad intervals around the
southern mainland perimeter of the harbor, the massive series of explosions would draw most—if not
all—soldiers and armaments outward, leaving us a
clear escape route across the harbor. And once the
blast went off, the Naval Academy would be without
lights or radio communication. And you could bet,
with Castro there, the whole damn Cuban army
would be moving in to defend it like hornets heading
for a trampled nest.

So I crawled on hands and belly, crossbow ready,
along the hedge of the cottage. Carefully, I edged
one eye over the ledge of window—and saw nothing.
Staying in the shadows, I moved around to the door,
cracked it, then swung it open.

The woman was gone, all right.

But her guard wasn't.

Poor Captain Zapata had suffered the final indignity. He lay bleeding on the floor, horribly cut. Androsa's blouse rested in shreds upon the bed. A chair
was overturned. The scenario became grimly clear: a
beautiful woman alone with the scorned soldier, so
he had tried to take her. And she had been lucky
enough to find a way to fight back—his own knife,

probably. So she had ruined him; killed him as he deserved to be killed, took his rifle and escaped. . . .

Took his rifle.

And suddenly the realization of what she would do next moved through me like a drug. The rustling in the bushes . . . and her promise to atone for the death of her brother, the murder of the three CIA agents, and her two years as a double agent. I didn't wait to move cautiously now. I threw myself away from the corpse of Zapata and the cottage, running fast, running low, headed for the clump of bushes which I knew sheltered Androsa Santarun.

But I was too late.

Just as I was about to dive for her, the AK-47 rattled orange flame, and beyond the window, the massive head of General Halcón disappeared like a bad dream while the silhouette of the dictator hesitated, then dove to safety.

I heard the screams of the guards and the sound of heavy footsteps running. I pulled her roughly out of the bushes. She was crying, sobbing hysterically.

"Androsa, Androsa, are you hurt . . . ?"

The guards were coming closer now. Somewhere someone fired wildly into the night.

"Androsa, are you all right?"

"I couldn't do it, Dusky, I couldn't. I had the gun on him but I couldn't—"

"Androsa, dammit, you did do it—Halcón's dead. Now we have to get the hell out of here."

Lights flared on all across the clearing. A guard running toward the cottage saw us, stopped, then swiveled to fire. I shoved myself down on top of her and took him cleanly with the Cobra, one gleaming arrow through the chest.

More soldiers were coming now. A siren blared. I took the remote-control detonator from my pocket and thumped back the cover.

It was now or never. I pulled Androsa down behind me into the cover of the wilderness mountainside. My foot hit something in the darkness and we both went tumbling into the safety of a gulley. Her face was hot and wet as I pulled her close against my chest. Still she sobbed, pouring out some strange confession that I couldn't quite comprehend and, finally, couldn't let myself believe.

". . . I . . . I wanted to kill him so badly, but back on the Isla de Pinos, when he was hiding in the mountains there—"

There was more gunfire now; soldiers shooting wildly. The place was getting hot as hell.

"Dammit, Androsa," I whispered hoarsely, "don't you think I've figured it out by now? The letter you left me was the final tip off; General Halcón was your father. So you killed him. He was one evil bastard, and now they're trying to kill us so stop that crying—"

"No!" There was a strange hysteria in her voice now. She took my face between her soft hands, peering at me in the darkness, making me listen to the unbelievable. "No, Dusky. You are so wrong. It is worse, much worse. It was not Halcón. No, I'm glad he is dead. But it is the other I should have killed.

But I couldn't! Dusky, Fidel Castro is my father! It is him I should have killed. . . .''

Too preoccupied to be shocked, I punched the button of the detonator roughly.

And that's when all hell broke loose. . . .

18

The bonefish moved over the flats in shafts of gray light, and the bottom was turtle grass and white sand and you could see the shadows of the fish as they traveled over the bottom in the clear water.

I stood at the window of my stilthouse watching them as they turned as one, slowed, then vectored to feed, throwing their milky wake. It was a glassy day in the decline of May; the expanse of shallow water moved away from my stilthouse swollen and metallic, shimmering in the distance with the quality of mirage.

"So who came out in the cruiser with you?"

I turned from the window and looked at Norm Fizer. His briefcase was on the table, papers spread before him. I tried to remember the last time I had seen him wearing something other than a suit—let alone something so casual as the brown tennis shorts and Bjorn Borg slipover shirt he wore now. Saigon, I decided. A rare day, that.

"Norm," I said, "I asked you who you brought out in the cruiser—"

"Dammit, Dusky, I *know* what you asked me." He smacked his pen down on the table in bad imitation of someone who is supposed to be mad. "I know because it's the third time you've asked me, and for the third time you'll find out when I get this damn report of yours straightened out—and I still can't figure out how you knew I brought someone out here with me."

I wagged my finger at him like a tolerant instructor. "Can't fool a fool, Stormin' Norman. Even tied to my stilthouse the way it is, the trim keeps shifting. Not much, but enough to tell me that Navy launch is either haunted or there's someone else with you."

"Okay," he said, frustrated. "I brought you a little surprise. Ever since you got back from Cuba you've been mooning around like some lovesick kid, and I decided to bring you a little something to cheer you up. You refused to let us fly you to the clinic in Washington, so I decided that to preserve your mental health I had to do something."

I crossed the plank floor of the stilthouse, yanked open the door of the gas fridge, got out two cold bottles of beer, and hunted for the opener. "Hey, you've dealt with those military headshrinkers before. They only want to know two things: why you hated your father, and the size of your . . . well, you know what. If that's analysis I can do without it."

"But you have been acting listless ever since—"

"The hell I have!" I said it too loud, the emotion blowing the credibility of the denial. Fizer hastened to cover his face with a big hand, trying to hide a smirk.

I plopped down in my baggy reading chair, put my feet up, and pulled at the beer. "Okay, okay," I said. "Let's get on with it—but I don't see why. I already filled out one report."

Norm shuffled through some papers. "Yeah, you filled out a report all right—the way one person fills the bleachers at Yankee Stadium. Here it is, and I quote: 'After detonating said diversion, the lieutenant in question accompanied me down the mountainside to Pier Three, where we convinced a captain in the Cuban army to transport us back to my boat via fast military launch."

"So that's what happened."

Fizer looked at me wryly. "But it does leave a few questions unanswered."

It did indeed. So I sat in the chair and fiddled with a new ultralight reel I had bought—a very fine German Quick with the asbestos drag system that might be the best made—and I told him about it.

The diversion had worked beautifully. The RDX explosives around the perimeter of the harbor had gone off with a massive *woof* and white glare that made the big searchlights seem pale in comparison. Our only tense moment was halfway down the mountain when the Cuban soldiers and sailors went pounding by us, headed for the Naval Academy like ants from a trampled nest. After that, we could have walked down the road to Pier Three singing and shouting. With no communication possible from the stone castle, Fidel Castro and his entourage were under heavy attack as far as the military around Mariel was concerned. It left the harbor wide open for our escape—once we found a boat fast enough and small enough to make it up the tidal creek to *Sniper*. And we had found one—one of the twin-engine patrol boats tethered to the quay surprisingly alone, but we had a visitor—Captain Lobo. After I treated him to a proper welcome—a few well-placed jabs that sent him crashing to the floor—he became very cooperative indeed, sniffling and whining and begging me not to kill him. He begged all the way back to Key West, where I turned him in.

Fizer scribbled in his report as I talked, big hands clumsy, seeming to balk at the secretarial work required of them. He looked up, paused and then said, "It's kind of surprising they didn't send some fighter planes after you once you made it back to your boat and headed for the States."

"Yeah," I said. "It is kind of surprising. Maybe with all the other American boats out there in the strait they didn't want to take a chance of strafing the wrong vessel. Or maybe they just didn't know it was me. But it was surprising."

It was, of course, a lie. Ten miles from international waters a big Cuban jet copter had come hovering over us, searchlights throwing a dazzling glare across *Sniper*. Immediately, Lobo recovered much of his surliness and went running to the aft deck waving his arms, expecting them to fire on the two Americans who had kidnapped him. But the assault never came. The chopper hovered above us as if awaiting orders, then banked away, back toward the mainland. Lobo was outraged. He couldn't understand it. But I did. Androsa, leaning against me as I stood at the controls, had told me about the Cuban revolutionary who, more than two decades before, had come down out of the mountains of the Isle of Pines to take a lover in the village on the Ensenada de Siguanea and how a girl child was born, and how he had abandoned the two of them to pursue what he was convinced was his destiny. Yet even after their years on diametrically opposed paths, he could not destroy the woman who was his daughter, and she could not kill the man behind the dictator she loathed. So only the three of us knew—or would ever know, because I had given her my word, and Fidel Castro sure as hell wasn't going to tell the world about the bastard child who had, in her own way, defeated him.

The voice of Norm Fizer brought me from my thoughts. "Another thing that isn't clear is why Lieutenant Santarun requested immediate duty in Europe. She was very vague about that." He eyed me slyly. "Did you have some kind of lovers' spat, or—"

"As I'm sure that goddam computer of yours up in Washington told you, the lady spent a week with me right here after our return. And it was a very pleasant week, and we did not quarrel." I shrugged. "Maybe she just didn't feel comfortable with all the new Cuban agents we have floating around this country thanks to the way the refugee exodus was handled."

And that was true. Castro was infamous for changing his mind. And if he reconsidered and decided he wanted another chance to see his daughter, it would be a simple matter . . .

Fizer stood up abruptly and checked his watch. "Well, Captain MacMorgan, I guess that just about does it. I've got a tennis date in Atlanta in . . . three hours, so I'd better get moving." He finished his beer in a gulp and began to stuff papers into his briefcase. "By the way," he said, "we turned over those two agents who posed as cameramen to an allied country of ours along with that Lobo character. I was rather surprised to learn there's a sizable community of ex-patriate Cubans living in London, and that the British had sent one of their agents from a Commonwealth island south of Cuba to . . ."

And that's when I heard the lumbering weight of him upon the steps of the stilthouse and heard the unmistakable brogue of his voice:

"Is it that ye think me some kind of a bloody suit that ya keep me closeted in that stinkin' motorboat o' yers, Captain Fizer?"

And he came clomping through the doorway, big Irish face flushed beneath the Viking beard, left arm in cast and sling, a patch of gauze taped to the side of his head.

"Jesus H. Christ!" I said, honestly stunned.

"No, 'tis only meself, brother MacMorgan—but close enough!"

Fizer had a wry smile on his face. "I believe you've met Captain Westy O'Davis, Dusky. Great Britain traded your three Cubans for this one Cayman agent—and frankly, I'm not sure we got the best of the bargain if he's as much like you as he seems."

"Hah!" The Irishman posed, offended, then marched over and gave me a bearlike slap on the shoulder. "I've come ta take ye up on your kind offer, Yank. This ugly brute of a friend o' yers says yer in need o' some recreation, so it's meself who have come ta lead ya in some beer drinkin', an' ta tell you some tall tales—an' did ya know there's a thousand bonefish feedin' right outside, one as big as God himself? It's true, Yank, it's true." He grinned at me and winked. "I swear it on the grave of me own dead mother. . . ."

Here's an exciting glimpse of the thrilling
adventure that awaits you in the next
novel of this action-packed series

THE DEADLIER SEX

Less than ten minutes after the props of my thirty-four-foot sportfisherman, *Sniper*, almost cut the girl into fish bait, the boat exploded.

Not my boat. Some kind of commercial trawler. Hard to tell for sure—there wasn't much left of it.

It went up with a dazzling flash and rumble on the near horizon, turning the full-moon night to eerie day and lighting the mangrove jungle shorelines of the Ten Thousand Islands in a Kodalith of stark whites and shadowed blacks. It was so unexpected that for one crazy moment I grabbed my head, thinking that I had been clubbed. But then, in the brightness of the explosion, I saw the burning four-foot wall of shock wave coming at us, and all we could do was hold fast and bow into it.

We were supposed to be on a vacation cruise. A little rest and recreation for me and a wild Irish friend of mine, Westy O'Davis. I had met O'Davis down in Mariel Harbor, Cuba. Mariel was an ideal place for making quick friends and influencing deadly enemies. The Irishman had, in a period of less than twenty-four hours, become a close friend. He also happened to have saved my life. Twice.

And he wasn't about to let me forget it.

So he had come to visit me on my little house built on stilts out on the clearwater flats of Calda Bank, near the pirate island of Key West. That's where I run *Sniper* out of as a charterboat. For years it was a valued way of life—working as a fishing guide, going down every morning to the docks at Garrison Bight where my sign reads:

> **Captain Dusky MacMorgan**
> **Billfish, Dolphin, Sharks, Grouper**
> **Full days, Half days—Inquire at Marina**

I didn't make much money as a fishing guide. But on the other side of the ledger, I had all the good, clear fishing days a man could want, pretty nice tourist people to show a good time to, and best of all, I was my own boss.

Once I also had a fine wife and twin boys who were the best of both of us. But then the drug pirates got them, and I had nothing.

So I went back to doing what I did best—the deadly trade I learned as a Navy SEAL. Revenge is not an ideal reason for living, but it's certainly one of the most compelling. And I have lived fully since.

Especially in Mariel Harbor, Cuba.

So, after that ordeal, it seemed reasonable that O'Davis and I take a little time off. O'Davis, who works for that labor-union-ruled island called Great Britain, is a leprechaun giant with red beard, copper hair, and a Viking face who speaks with the amused black humor of the Irish poet. O'Davis had gone to Mariel from his island home in the Caymans, where his cover occupation includes leading scuba diving tours and squiring around the pretty tourist ladies.

But he had had enough of government work and killing, and so had I, so we had spent that first week on my stilthouse drinking cold beer, battling good fish on light tackle, and telling tall tales. Then one night, while I sat with beer, a good book, and a fresh dip of Copenhagen, O'Davis began to go through my library of Florida charts. He unrolled them one by one, studying them, humming some strange tune as he did. I watched his broad face in the yellow light of the kerosene lamp.

"I want those all rolled back and catalogued the way I had them, O'Davis."

"Tum-da-dum-dum-dum . . . what?" And when I repeated it, he made a face of mock outrage. "An' do ya' think me some kind of slovenly child, Dusky MacMorgan, that ya' be remindin' me to care for yer precious charts?"

"I do."

"Hah! An' now yer laughin' at me to boot!" He made as if to throw down the chart he was holding, then thought better of it. "So this is the thanks I get for savin' the life of the likes of you—and a big, ugly brute you are, too. . . ."

"Oh god, O'Davis."

"I'll wager ya didn' think me a slovenly child when meself, Westy O'Davis, clouted the Cuban guard who was about ta shoot ya. . . ."

"Do I have to listen to this again?"

"An' knocked the bloody Russian rifle from the other guard's hands . . ."

"O'Davis?"

". . . jest when he was about ta' shoot ya, ye ugly little snit . . ."

"O'Davis. Just tell me why you're looking at the charts, okay?"

He stopped in mid-sentence, looked at me, and grinned. It was the kind of pleasant banter we had been enjoying all week; the kind the big Irishman reveled in. He rattled the chart meaningfully and said grandly, "Because, brother MacMorgan, tomorrow we're gettin' on that black-hulled power demon of yers and takin' a trip. All week long ye've been tellin' me that the only coastal wilderness left in Florida is the southwest coast, an' now that I've seen the Ten Thousand Islands on the chart, I want to see them in real life."

I shrugged, hiding my enthusiasm. Truth was, my stilthouse is awfully close quarters for two big men. And I, like the Irishman, was getting a little antsy. Besides, I loved the Ten Thousand Islands and the wilderness below them. On a map of Florida, it looks like the area below Naples and that concrete grotesquerie called Marco Island breaks into a massive jigsaw puzzle of windswept islands and sea. It's wild and deserted—a hundred miles of tidal rivers and mangrove islands and stretches of desolate beach.

"Bugs will be bad," I said.

"Devil take the bugs."

"I have a friend who lives on one of the backcountry islands. He's a hermit."

"The island with all the tarpon?"

I nodded. "But there'll be no women, O'Davis. Don't forget that. You're not going to be able to slip into Key West like you did last night and cat around."

He put on his special lecherous look and winked at me. "After last night, who needs the ladies, brother MacMorgan? I felt like a candle in a town full of moths, I did—so who needs 'em now?"

So that's how we happened to be cruising off White Horse Key on a full-moon night in June. It had taken us three very lazy days of fishing and diving to get across Florida Bay and idle our way along Cape Sable and past the mangrove giants of Shark River. We had spent the best of the twilight nosing around Indian Key Pass on the outgoing tide, taking five good snook on sweetened jigs and releasing four. So now I steered from the main controls of the cabin, vectoring in on the distant flare of Coon Key light with the vague idea of running into the backcountry, where the tarpon would be rolling in sheens of silver moonlight by the old houseboat across from Dismal Key.

Because of the bright moon, we ran without lights. The VHF was off in favor of a Fort Myers radio station that fed a steady diet of classic old jazz throughout *Sniper*. O'Davis was up on the flybridge, supposedly watching for crabpot buoys that could foul *Sniper*'s twin brass wheels. But he was actually gazing at the moon, drinking beer, and singing. It is the secret belief of most ethnic descendants that those little ethnic legends are full-blown truths, as if some mystic source seeds our brains with the talents of ancient birthright. With Italians it is cooking, with the French it is love, with the Swedes it is sailing, and with the Irish it is singing. I don't know about the Italians, French, and Swedes, but Westy O'Davis was seriously shortchanged in his atavistic talents. His Irish tenor sounded more like a water spaniel having difficulties with a bear. Even so, he still loved to sing— and that's really why he was up on the flybridge.

I was relaxed, listening to the strains of vintage Cole Porter waft across water and airwaves, studying the hulking shadow of mainland coast. *Sniper* was running a conservative twenty knots, and the silver expanse of sea spread out before us. It was a good night to sip at a cold beer and enjoy the nocturnal desolation only the sea and certain northern forests can offer, and I was caught up in the beauty of it all when the roaring voice of O'Davis snapped me out of my reverie.

"Back 'er, Dusky! Back 'er *now*, Yank!"

At sea you don't question a command like that—and back her I did, driving both gearshifts into abrupt reverse, cringing at the strain I knew was being put on the transmission. There was a slight *clunk* against the fiberglass hull, then nothing. I switched the engines off, then went running back to the aft deck.

"What the hell did you see, you crazy—"

"There's someone out there, Yank!" He pointed anxiously to port. "Someone swimmin'—I swear it. Thought it was a bloody dog at first!"

And then I saw it too. A dark shadow on the silver veil of water. Someone clinging to something. Someone weak, floundering. And disappearing rapidly astern as the momentum of *Sniper* carried us onward. In one long step I was on the transom, quickly diving head-long into the night sea. I swam with head up, keeping a close eye on the dark shape in the distance. Behind me, I heard O'Davis start *Sniper* and turn to follow.

It was a person all right. Someone hanging on to one of those cheap weekender life vests. The Coast Guard says the vests are fine for pleasure craft. And they are—if said pleasure craft doesn't sink. I tried shouting, and got a low moan for an answer. So I made a quick forward approach, grabbed a dangling arm, pulled and took the chin firmly in my right hand, then switched to a cross-chest carry with my left.

And that's when I realized my victim was a woman. A very, very naked woman.

O'Davis came up carefully behind us, reversed engines expertly, and rigged the boarding ladder. I slung her over my shoulder in a fireman's carry and pulled her up onto *Sniper*. He had a blanket ready, and I put her down back first on the deck. The cabin lights were on and you could see her clearly. She looked about twenty or twenty-one, though she could have been a few years older. Blond hair, cut as short as a boy's, surrounded a fine, angular face with a strong nose and full mouth. She was short— all breasts and shoulders, with slender hips and thin legs. No rings. No necklace. And not a stitch. O'Davis quickly pulled the blanket up around her—an admirable show of character because, as they say in the commercials, she was a very full-figured girl.

"Do ye know first aid, Yank?" We stood shoulder to shoulder, staring at the girl wrapped in the blanket. *Sniper*'s engines burbled quietly in the moonlight, and somewhere a wading bird squawked.

"I do for drowning—but she wasn't drowning. She had a life vest. I think we may have clipped her with the hull when we went by."

O'Davis knelt and gently searched the fine blond hair with his meaty hand. "Aye. There's a lump here, sure enough." He looked up at me. "What in bloody hell do ya think she was doin' at midnight a quarter-mile off shore in the Ten Thousand Islands?"

I shook my head. "Damned if I know. Maybe she was on a boat that went down. Or went for a swim and got caught by the tide. It happens."

The Irishman picked her up and carried her down

into the forward vee-berth. She moaned softly, stretched her neck as if to yawn, then opened her eyes. The shock registered when she realized she was on a strange boat, and both hands strained to pull the blanket tightly around her body. "Hey! Where am I? Who are you? What in the hell do you—"

"Shush . . . shush now, child," O'Davis said gently. He reached to pat her head, and she jerked violently away.

"Keep your rotten hands off me!" She threw herself back on the bunk, twisting her head away.

I looked at the Irishman. "Like moths to a candle flame, huh?"

"Ah, she's young, Yank. Very young. But give 'er time and she'll be baskin' in me light."

"Well, we're not going to give her much time because I'm calling the Coast Guard right now and having them send out a helicopter. A head injury is nothing to toy with—"

"No!" It was the girl, sitting up again, a wild look in her eyes. "No, don't call the Coast Guard. Please—"

I didn't have time to ask her why she didn't want me to notify the Coast Guard. Because that's when the sea turned to fire. The mangroves a quarter-mile away were caught in a stark-white light—the same fiery light that showed me the shock wave rolling toward us.

That's when the boat—less than 800 yards away—suddenly exploded, lighting *Sniper* in its orange chromosphere, and catching the half-smile on the face of the girl. . . .

Randy Wayne White
writing as Randy Striker

THE DEEP SIX

When a well-known eccentric scavenger in Key West shows Dusky MacMorgan a golden chain, it's no ordinary trinket—it's the key to finding a treasure at the bottom of the sea. Before MacMorgan can find out where that is, the eccentric vanishes off his boat, the apparent victim of a shark attack. But MacMorgan suspects the true killer walked on two legs. Surrounded by predators in and out of the water who are armed with both brute strength and breathtaking beauty, he's going hunting for the treasure— and for vengeance.

"White takes us places that no other Florida mystery writer can hope to find."
—Carl Hiassen

0-451-21970-8

Available wherever books are sold or at
penguin.com

SIGNET

Randy Wayne White writing as Randy Striker

"Raises the bar of the action thriller."
—Miami Herald

KEY WEST CONNECTION

Ex-Navy SEAL Dusky MacMorgan survived a
military hell only to find it again where he least
expects it—as a fisherman trolling the Gulf stream
in his thirty-foot clipper. His new life is shattered
when a psychotic pack of drug runners turns the
turquoise waters red with the blood of his beloved
family. Armed with an arsenal so hot it could blow
the Florida coast sky-high, he's tracking the goons
responsible—right into the intimate circle of a
corrupt U.S. senator living beyond the law in his
own island fortress. But now it has to withstand the
force of a one-man hit-squad.

0-451-21801-9

Available wherever books are sold or at
penguin.com